Nikos Engonopoulos

Poems

Translated by
Manolis Aligizakis

Translation copyright © Manolis Aligizakis, 2025
Published in 2025 by Libros Libertad Publishing Ltd
2244 154A Street, Surrey B.C. V4A 5S9
All rights reserved.

Library and Archives Canada Cataloguing in Publication
Title: Poeme / Poems
by Nikos Engonopoulos

Translated by Manolis Aligizakis
Selection of the poems: Manolis Aligizakis
Cover design by Iryna Spica

ISBN 978-1-926763-73-6

Printed in the US by Amazon/Kindle

Contents

Foreword

I first heard about surrealism many years ago, during my army years, when a friend and soldier in the same company with me brought out of his pocket a note he had written, which he read to me during our short break from the daily exercises. His poetics seemed different from what I knew up to that time, much to his amusement, and he rushed to tell me it was surrealistic poetry, a movement well-known to poetic circles of the era but not as much to me. He said it was the *new wave*, the term we used to describe the new way music was produced those days and poetry was written, as I found out. My friend also named two prominent surrealist poets, Andreas Embirikos and Nikos Engonopoulos.

I, up to that time, was familiar with the Nobel Prize winners, George Seferis, Odysseus Elytis, Constantine Cavafy, Yannis Ritsos, Tasos Livaditis, and a few others mostly poets whose works were set in music, something common those days and also with poets we studied at school, Solomos, Palamas, Drosinis, Kalvos, and a few others who were included in the school curriculum. I didn't know Nikos

Engonopoulos and the other surrealist Andreas Embirikos at all. The poetic formats I was familiar with were revised, new ways of stanza structuring appeared plus the strange way of imagery made me a little uncomfortable, I very much liked the idea of these new poetics which were mostly known as the opposition to traditional formats, the rhyming verse, and the old austere Katharevousa language, and as such, because they stood opposite the old ways of writing I felt a keen attraction to it.

A few years later and after my release from the army and my emigration to Canada, I met another Hellene with a vast collection of music of that era, among which he had an album, called Bolivar, which introduced me again to surrealist poetry through the music which I loved from the acoustic point of view but also from the imagery, which I started to understand better. Then it occurred to me that the beauty of surrealistic verse was its spontaneity and from the gut, sort of originating format that slowly got into me in an unprecedented way. I also loved Bolivar, the symbol which was known to the whole world and which I remember from my years in high school and university when we used to recite every revolutionary verse we could find, especially during the years of dictatorship in Hellas between 1967 and 1973 when I emigrated to Canada.

Nikos Engonopoulos's daughter Errietti recalled her father's last years when she lived close to him after he retired and she was allowed to visit her dad's atelier, *"he was a man who knew how to talk to a young child, he could enter my world and stir my interest. While he was still alive, I typed all his handwritten works. After his passing I discovered a piece of work half typed, half handwritten. It consisted of 4-5 translations and a few prose pieces, which I passed to his publisher. I have always been awed by his work and these days I realize that interest in surrealism has been reignited. The revolution that that movement represented was very important to many people and for this reason, I decided to do my best that everything he wrote will be made available to the public. Such creators with such an innovative presence, like my father, are rare in our era."*

Nikos Engonopoulos' poetry was in my plans for a translation. I realized there weren't many such books available for English poetry lovers, so I decided to try. I appreciate Errietti's gracious permission. I hope my work represents a good rendition of her father's excellent work, and I also hope poetry lovers over the globe will appreciate this book.

Manolis Aligizakis, Cretan, author, poet, translator

Introduction

Nikos Engonopoulos was born on October 21st, 1907, and died on 31 of October 1985. He's still almost unknown in the Hellenic School books except for a few excerpts from his famous poem Bolivar since no one ever talks of men who stood against oppression and subjugation, subjects untouched by any literary circle or educational forums. Early in his life, he felt a powerful connection to the Byzantine era with its art, which fascinated him for its traditional and esthetic values but also because of his wish to discover his way of expression since he wanted not only to appear as modern but at the same time as purely Hellenic. He surely wrote about the Byzantine era, but he also painted. He was established first as a painter, as he underscored himself, however, and later as a poet although he was passionate about both artistic forms.

As a poet, he appeared for the first time in 1938 with his book *Don't Talk to the Driver* which was utterly rejected by the established poetic circles of Athens which acted the way literary circles often react to a newcomer with a new vision or a new poetic format. The collection created a fuss and fierce resistance as it reached the level of literary scandal. Most critics ridiculed him, the same as they did with Andreas Embirikos, and considered his work more as a wordplay rather than poetry with depth. His only supporter was the surrealist Embirikos who wrote *Nikos Engonopoulos there are just two important concepts in this world, Eros and the Sword. All else follows them and last in importance are the critics. You are a truly great poet, let them say as they wish.*

Although he published his second poetry book *The Clavichord of Silence*, a year later he only started being recognized some twenty years later when he was awarded the National Literary Prize for his book *On a Flowery Hellenic Logos*. He was also awarded the same award in 1979 for his book *In the Valley with the Rose Gardens*. In 1944 he presented his Bolivar, his most exceptional work, which was received with a lukewarm reaction. It was published during the destructive Second World War and the fresh scars it had inflicted upon humanity; however, it was received with an optimistic view as the liberator Bolivar was a hero who transcended time and locale and was perceived as the new ray of hope amid the despair that blanketed the world.

Bolivar begins with recognizing the seriousness that prompted the poet to write such a work: Bolivar, the name made of steel and wood, you were a flower in the gardens of South America. Then, the poet first identified himself with the famous freedom fighter of the Americas and made him the Hellenic hero of the 1821 revolution against the occupiers, the Turks, *for the austere and beautiful faces of Odysseus Androutsos and Simon Bolivar.*

The local hero turns universal, and he belongs not only to Hydra *Bolivar! I cry out your name, lying on the top of*

Mount Ere, the highest peak on Hydra Island and the islands of the Saronicos Bay and Africa and from Panama to the tip of South America and even Mexico: *but to Panama, Guatemala, Nicaragua, Honduras, Haiti, San Domingo, Bolivia, Columbia, Perou, Venezuela, Chile, Argentina, Brazil, Paraguay, Ecuador, even to Mexico.* This is the hero who transcends borders, and this is the one the poet sings about. Then the poet localizes the hero and brings him to the Hellenic lands, *Bolivar, you are beautiful like a Hellene.* The poet's love for the Byzantine Era appears here as he immortalizes his first encounter with the hero in, *as a child, I first met you on an uphill side street of Phanari.* Then the hero truly becomes a Hellene *Bolivar, you are the son of Rigas Feraios, and of Antony Economou, who so unjustly they slaughtered.*

The poet perceives the concept of the hero as an indisputable benevolence that people aspire to and school children dream of becoming, it overpowers pneuma and logic and turns into the symbol; the hero transcends borders and from the local person becomes the universal symbol everyone admires and narrates his accomplishments. In the poem The Ruler of Karytaina, the poet speaks of a foreigner in Morea, Peloponnese, during the 14th century who was admired and respected by his populace because he was a *diaphanous* man and a clear sou. The wonders who the man is,

> *who is he who raised a warring staff and walked*
> *the whole night and he dwelled in bogs*
> *who is he that in the foggy noon of sadness*
> *he fought against the world and was victorious,*

then proceeds to establish the hero as a content man who dwells in the power of his silence,

hearts ploughed by the pain of love
eyes gruesomely furrowed by the lustful longing
the viscera he uprooted he will sow into the winds
and like an avenger, he will stand on the Silent Castle

After *Bolivar*, the poet reappears with his book *The Return of the Birds, Eleusis, The Atlantic, On a Flowery Hellenic Logos,* which slowly established him as a unique voice, which his good friend Andreas Embirikos expresses his love and admiration for the poet crystallized with his commentary, *Nikos Engonopoulos or the Miracle of Elbasan and Bosporus* with the words, His rapturous, vigilant, pulsing and fiery passion lights the emotional space that creates and unfolds his imagery.

Various elements are evident in the works of the poet known for his transcendental thinking, for his mostly analytical mind, the revolutionary poet, uncontrolled by established formats and modes and insubordinate to every external ideological border. He is a Hellene poet and a universal one. He draws his imagery from the endless richness of the Hellenic Landscape, the ancient beauty of Byzantium, and the Hellenic revolution of 1821.

Beauty and its power are a crucial detail he often refers to, as he sees it everywhere, in the Kore lying on her deathbed,

the beautiful Kore
we loved,
oh, mister,
was like
a cyclamen
on her death
bed,

even in the gypsies with their transient lifestyle, the people who never believed in spreading roots anywhere, but they constantly move from place to place, *let us drive the gypsies to the sea*, who he suggests must try and move to different lands beyond the seas, the n he concludes that Eros, lust should be the driving force in every human,

let us harvest the breasts
of our most beautiful
girls.

He loves every frontrunner, every creator of something new, and he identifies with each of those persons since he also, being a surrealist, is a creator of new forms of expression to show his affection for such creators he wrote a long poem with the title, Picasso, the cubist painter whose works he truly loved, the poem written in both Hellenic and French is his dedication to the great Spanish creator of cubism, a new painting format that rejected traditional techniques and instead emphasized the two-dimensional surface of the canvas. Cubist paintings are fragmented and abstracted, breaking objects down into geometric forms and showing multiple views of a subject at once. This new technique captivated Engonopoulos who dedicated a whole poem to the famous Spanish creator which describes a bullfight, although the scene starts at a Hellenic locale,

the matador after all lives in Ellassona
by the cobblestone square under the plane trees
and the café owner goes back and forth refilling
his cup of coffee and the smoke of his narghile

The poet recalls Hellenic scenes of a mother fighting fascism, of knotty hands and hanging dry peppers which the poet quite elaborately unfolds,

> *and the mother who wants to stop the fascists*
> *inside the dark room where the plotters discuss things*
> *and peppers dry up hanging from the ceiling*
> *with her knotty hands, adorned with rings,*

the scene then transfers to Spain and the arena where the drama takes place with gypsy girls dancing,

> *the gypsy girls with wide pelvis and fluttering,*
> *colourful loosened dresses,*

and with the bull striking and spreading death in his passing

> *and a mountain of bodies were piled*
> *bodies of men and horses*
> *in rivers of blood*
> *finally,*

and ultimately death is defeated with rebirth, images of girls with beautiful breasts lie on their backs and procreation takes place

> *and girls with the beautiful breasts lay down*
> *on their backs*
> *and suns go down and rise,*
> *in their beautiful eyes*

The image of death's defeat by the newborn baby is also described in Odysseus Elytis' poem Axion Esti, where he refers to the four great voids, *the void of the Death for the Coming Infant, the void of Murder for the Just Judgment, the void of sacrifice for the Equal Compensation the void of Soul for the Responsibility of the Others.*

An abundance of images and clear descriptions fill these poems with a variety of subjects and themes the reader encounters, such as the point of education, when one wonders why contemporary education teaches the students enough so that they understand, accept and believe what they were taught but never much more to the point of reaching the level of knowledge that affords them the capability to question what they were taught, *// But how, oh, Lord, can you forget the sorry state of your Creation?* Further on the poet touches on the sensitive vein of morality and like a new Nietzsche he wonders about the value of morality, *no, no, an endless morality won't help us change the world into a better one,* he also touches another sensitive vein of society by questioning the value people lay on second-hand values, banality, and acceptance of societal modes which never lead man to a better-higher lifestyle (higher in a psychospiritual way) but only to the mediocrity of peons, *into dried-up bacalao hanging off the middle mast to replace the flags of many boring fanaticisms.* There are certainly many poems that refer to the benevolent effect of love and its role in the life of man,

> *you'll never stop calling up all the love*
> *you have hidden inside you, against the forces of evil*

Nikos Engonopoulos passed at the age of 78 in October 1985 from a heart attack. He was laid at the 1st Cemetery of Athens. His artistic works are considered among the important surrealist poetry of modern Hellas along with the works of Andreas Embirikos to whom Nikos Engonopoulos often refers. His poetry is set apart for its personal use of the language, his abundant symbolism, and his ability to transpose images from various locales of the globe to the Hellenic landscape thus transcending space and time that creates a timeless and borderless totality. His contribution to modern Hellenic poetry is unparalleled and signifies the unique expression of Hellenism.

Don't Talk to the Driver

1938

Tram and Acropolis

Le soleil me brule et me rend lumineux

in the monotonous rain
the mud
the ashy atmosphere
trams go by
and through the
deserted agora,
that the rain rendered dead,
they go to
their destinations

my thought
filled with emotion
follows them tenderly until
they reach
the end of the line
where the fields start
that the rain drowns

how sad it would be, my God,
what a sorrow
unless my heart didn't console me
the hope of the marbles
and the expectation of a bright sunray
that would give new life
to the exquisite ruins

exactly like
the red flower
among the green leaves

Don't Talk to the Driver

while dancing, Albanians think to focus their energies
toward new directions, so that their children won't feel
anything about their struggles, disappointments, and
bitter life. They won't sense anything before they
mature. In any case, these thoughts of the Albanians
never cross the frames of their windows. And this, since
an Italian, named Guglielmo Tzitzi, a repairman of wind
instruments tried to fool the newlyweds, applied on
an old Singer sewing machine with four pipes, two
of them made of glass and the other two made of any
metal. Don't any of you be concerned: this image is the
only one that helped the dead blind lighthouse guard
to discover the secret of the artesian well.

II

(*About Winds and Waters*)

eternal memory to the master, the Kindest Ottoman
Ali Hantzar, a servant of the Empire, the great world
Benefactor, helped by the Italian Guglielmo Tzitzi.
This was also the opinion of Madam Artemis, whose
Confirmation consoles the wandering souls and greatly
contributes to the efforts of the sixteenth-century French
poets who tried to create the New School named
the Pleiades. Besides none of us forgets that the monk
Schwartz discovered gunpowder. Thus, for the rest ...

Gas

in the forest
among the thick branches
the light reaches
from the heavy sky
close to the soil
blanketed
by rotten leaves
a bird is perched
on a low branch

a very
strange
bird: looks
plucked
thoughtful

an old bird

what this old bird
may be thinking
in the darkness?

Ah, nothing
it thinks of nothing!

Simply
it has a guilty
passion
for her

Lotus

where are we led
by the fear
of feathers
when the psalms of crowbars
disrupt
the fine life of Parthenon
or perhaps the green mirror
the simplest green, velvet mirror
is enough
to stop
the sobs
the rhythmic and subdued sobs
of underground
steel bars?

drop
jaw
melting pot
silence

Tel Aviv

Eleanor
the golden girl
played the harp
with her beautiful
white
hands

yet no sound
was heard
from the harp

all the music
was
in her beautiful eyes
among her green hair

from the harp, though,
one after the other
came a bird
a green soap bar
and
an iron
a prevalent one
exactly what
Zyiotes,
during a storm,
call
Ars Amantis

Praise under the Rain

I

let us give something to the Theresia of Jesus Christ
let us give something to the great poet
let us give something to Pablo Picasso

but let us give nothing
to the black mouths of water wells
to the worthy of tears Bactrian camels
to the dark clocks of war

II

the beautiful Kore
we loved,
oh, mister,
was like
a cyclamen
in her death
bed
let us dust off our muddy pants
let us stir the harps of artesian wells
let us drive the gypsies to the sea
let us harvest the breasts
of our most beautiful
girls

Marines

they killed kindly, as it was supposed to,
that big lady
inside the bright décor
of yellow precious silks

for these
and the forgotten bottles of pop in carafes
and the nice, nostalgic stories of that fool
they were nothing but moans of lust
to the wells
to the plains
to the kite

Polyxeni

frosty auras brought to me shouting vampires
yesterday, towards midnight, when the sun of
justice was midair, the message of Dante Gabriel
Rosetti, of the Isidore Ducasse* and Panagis
Koutalianos. My sadness was great. Up to that time
I believed in the prophetic visions of the machinists,
I longed for the oracles of other-minded horse riders,
I anticipated the metaphysical interventions of
the statues. The idea of my corpse felt serene. My
only joy was the locks of her hair. I'd bow down and
kiss the edge of her toes. Still a kid, during the sundown,
I ran like a madman to steal, before night fell, the
forgotten scarecrows from the fields. However, I lost her
for good, I'd say from my hands as if she wasn't but
a foolish dream, a regular hammer. In her place was
only a mirror. And when I leaned and looked in this
mirror, I didn't see anything else but two small stones:
one of them was labelled Polyxeni and the other, also
Polyxeni.

---

*   *Compte de Lautreamont*

Osiris

Late in the night, in the higher neighbourhoods, wild and bloodthirsty Albanians, seven of them, mercilessly slaughtered, on his bed, the dog-headed lover of the forgotten Hippolyta. The senseless murderers entered without being seen by anyone, into the room of the horrible killing. After they hymned with their flutes two unknown hymns to me, two hymns for the hoopoes, they carefully placed under a glass containing a diluted fish glue mixed with a light dose of nitroglycerine, a piece of paper. A common correspondence paper with a written note: "Golden Column" After that, the killers left the house unseen again. The dog-headed lover, let us call him thus since his name Isidor was unknown to us, left the tragic room much later. He was wearing a grey overcoat and glasses.

Ship of the Forest

I know that
if I had
an attire,
a suit,
green colour, open
with dark red flowers

if in the place
of the invisible
Aeolian harp I use
as my head
I had a square bar
of green soap
so that it could touch
softly
one of its edges
between my two shoulders

if it is possible
to replace
the holy shrouds
of my voice
with the love
the metaphysical musical Kore
has for
the black umbrellas

perhaps then
only then
I could name

that the fleeting
visions of joy
I had once seen,
when I was a child,
looking
reverently
inside the round
eyes
of birds

Road Roller

My heart is made of solid rubber, pierced by
two worthless, painful nails. I take it and although
it resists with its hands and legs I manage by force
to hide it in a drawer, where I secretly keep words and
stories from the land of bicycles. I'm not afraid of the
phallus-carrying virgin or the man with the fur eyes
who goes up and down the dark stairs. I've known
the mirror of flowers since my childhood. I sing to the
glories of road rollers, the pure hymns of the bottles, as
the paper owl, with its cone, says straight into my ear
the word, *Foreign*

This Memory

now that the nightmare of fans has vanished
now that the pedophiles kick the shore
let us turn our glance
to the architectural despair

only that time
hasn't come yet
only the musical sponges
have come and
the crazy snail

and one Cappadocian came
from San Salvador and had
two salted fish instead of eyes

Eleanor

*for hands, she hath non, nor
eyes, or feet, or golden
treasure of hair*

(*front view*)

her hair is of carton
and like a fish
her two eyes are
like a dove
her mouth
is like a civil war
(in Spain)
her neck is a red
horse
her hands
are
like the voice
of thick forest
her two breasts are
like my paintings
her belly is
the history
of Velthandros and Chrysantza
the story
of Tobias
the story
of a donkey
of the wolf and fox
her gender

is
sharp whistles
in the quietness
of noon
her thighs are
the last
gleams
of timid joy
of the road rollers
her two knees
Agamemnon
her two reverent
small
feet
are the green
telephone
with the red eyes

(*rear view*)

her hair
is
the oil lamp
that burns
in the morning
her shoulders
are
the hammer
of my lust
her back is
the binoculars
of the sea

the plough
of the foolish
inscriptions
whistles
sadly
on her waist
her buttocks
are
fishbones
saddened
her thighs
are
like
a thunderbolt
her small heals
light
the bad dreams
in the mornings

and finally
she is
a woman
half hippocampus
and half
necklace
perhaps even
part cypress
and partly
an elevator

Amazons

The beautiful Marica Politissa, was the only goddaughter of Pope Innocent the VIII. He was a young child then, perhaps not even born yet. She was already married, the wife of the hegemonic house of Artavazos Shyriktropoulos, nephew, via his sister, of Noah. However, this murder couldn't be left without a severe, exemplary punishment. Indeed, the next day, an order was given to many ships to sail quickly to the Canary Islands and Fiji to collect as many clouds as possible, lies, forgotten memories, deadly sins and phonograph pins, perhaps made in England. These seven ships were: four sails, twelve crafts, two royal caravels and one dead engaged woman. The fleet passed under my window early in the morning. They sang a beautiful, although sad hymn. Still today, I vaguely recall its tune: it was better than the bell tune, although worse than a broom.

Tradition

A wolf, by the stairs, howls sorrowfully. And it is I
or better it is my heart that has longed, for years now,
for the coming of Sardanapalus, in the form of either a
dynamite fuse or a joyous flower. I enjoy my boredom
reading chapters of *fish* among the sexual documents
of lotus-eaters. However, I sense around the ballooned
disgust and enmity of the clergy. They accused me of
being due respect by a group of strange omnivorous
red-skinned fishers. Local ship magnates and tennis
players of both genders stigmatized me as the brainy
bicycle of Hittites. They accused me of murder and
that I kicked, in my rage, the holy bone of dinosaurs.
However, I'm serene. Serenity and quietness reign in
my soul, although it has rained since morning. They
all shout at me:
> give yourself up!

But I don't. It's enough for me I give English lessons
twice or three times a week to the local sewing
machines of the embrasures. They all shout at me:
> give yourself up!

No, I'll only give the frozen king the hexagon fireworks
of the guillotines. They all shout at me:
> give yourself up!

Ok, I'll surrender. Let it be. But why? Am I or not
involved in the night killing? Am I or not the shouting
plough, the crocodile gasoline? Am I or not the fiery
helmet of a leather expert, the enemy of thunderbolts?
But since I realized that my life was the fuse of the lamp,
a word, the electric switch of Aramaic piano keys of
silence, for this reason
> I give myself up!

Perhaps

It rains ... yet I'm sorry to tell you: there was, here,
a house, a huge, gigantic house. It was deserted. There
were no windows; it had two balconies and one big
chimney. A girl with no eyes was sitting there; instead
of a voice, she had a flower. She asked me:
"Why did you nail so many nails in the morning?"
"Oh, nothing, I was just talking to Homer"
"Homer the poet?"
"Yes, the poet and another Homer from Moshopolis,
who spent all his life on trees, like a bird, yet he was
known as the *man of the bridge* around the lake
neighbourhoods"

Love

We are leaving. But before we say goodbye, let us
all sing the song of the *stone* car. And when I say *stone*
I mean, it has stones only at the corners, the rest is
made, as usual, from bricks and planks and the wheels
are painted with iodine. Let us keep the memory of the
radial maze and the step pebbles of the incendiary boxes.
Like any other time, let us turn to the right toward the lit
ruins of our love. Memory and wish of the asphalt:
Poseidon. For me, a star in a drawer sang my joy song
for a saw. No one should follow. We all, like mythological
chandeliers and like metal lightning conductors, let us
rest. Along with the birds, with a bird, with two birds.

There

The net-like inexistent fans
of forgetfulness
were the only
consolation
among the blood
of a virgin
who never mentioned her name
among the songs
of the gray substance
in the red fine winds

yet it was meant
between the hooks
the wheels
the springs
and the tears
of the young whale
to sprout, just like that,
a fico tree
that decorated
the poor hall

voices
and the unmade tragic beds
of spasms

Mystic Poet

hommage à ravel

shadow of the lake
spread in the room
and under the chair
even under the table
behind the books
and in the dark glances
of the gypsum models
the song of
secret orchestra
of the dead poet
then the woman entered
who I was waiting
for a long time
naked
dressed in white
under the bright moonlight
with loosened hair
and some yellow grass in her eyes
that undulated slowly
like promises
never made
in faraway unfamiliar cities
and in empty
deserted
factories

and I felt like vanishing
like the dead poet

among her long hair
and some flowers
that bloom
at night
and shut
in the morning
and like some dry fish
they hanged
with a string
high up
in the coal storage room

thus, I'll go
far away
from the people's buzz
and the noise
of the shooting range
to go far away
among the broken
windows
and to live
forever
on the ceiling
yet always
having
in my eyes
the secret songs
of the dead orchestra
of the poet

The Airport Wooden Effigies

they left forever
far away from us
the stones of the East
epithalamic dead crocodiles
in the palace
the sewing machines
painted yellow
and now, they remain, and forever,
like airtight conclusions
of the finest Ithaca
from the hermetic chisels
of father killers
so that, the dirty bedsheets of sacrifice
wake up deep
inside of me,
when I laugh

like the forest that will be consoled
by the sperm
of asleep fishes
between the lips
it asks for the systemic oils of life
and sings only one song
the youths sang in the dark side street
about the velvety corals
of the eyes

Maria of the Night

next day after my death, or rather my execution, I took all the newspapers so that I may learn as much as possible about it. It seems they lead me to the gallows under the protection of a serious group of guards. I was wearing, they said, a yellow overcoat, a rope around my neck and a helmet. My hair was like a brush, a painter's or that of a pine-bender. Then, they threw my corpse away, in a bog, in the French Cartesian's hideaway and into where, there was, for years, food for the beasts and a hierodule, named Euterpe, the corpse of forever known Karamanlakis, and although many things were said in secret, around those days I was, for some of them in Maracaibo, in South America and for some others in Piraeus, at Passalimani, while I was in Elbassan in Albania. And the only important thing that I read those days, was a long letter from the Italian Gulielmos Tsitzis, my only friend, who, certainly, I have never met and who I don't believe ever existed. In short, the whole letter was the following: "You are he'd say, meaning Polyxeni, of course, an old gramophone with a brass cone under a black cloth".

The Clavichords of Silence

1939

Sinbad the Sailor

My soul is often
a side street in Mykonos
in the twilight
and women start
putting down on the street,
quite erotically and
in triangular, monotonous shapes
blue glasses
blue plates
blue carafes
blue lust
violins
flowers
pebbles
all in blue colour
away from the sun
on the soil
in the street
where the sun passed
besides
it won't pass again

then exactly then
is the time
when I
pass my hand
softly
over my cranium
and I press it
deep

in my head
and I pull out
my brain
and squeeze serenely
my grey substance
between
my fingers

and when all
the fluid
is drained
without any words
onto the soil
only a flower
is left in
my palm
which flower
I seek since
my childhood
and which caresses
my forehead with
its white
hands
and talks to me
tenderly
and talks
about the dreams
that whistle in the night
so ever quietly
so passionately
like fingers
like tears

among the ruins
of Palmyra
in the dead palaces
of Babylon

and it still talks to me
about the life
I live quietly
serenely
in the huge
empty house
made completely of blue
into which
only birds live
I all alone
motionless
among the electric
wires of Her belly

and during the storm's wrath
outside and
the deck
of my deserted ship
is covered
by the angry sea
I, barefoot,
climb up the mast
holding tightly
in my hands
a glass
made of blue

with these hands
my forehead
that isn't burnt
by the lightning bolts
and the eagles
are this blue
 glass
into which
I poured
the fluids that fell
off my hands
the small flower
and even a long
very long
blue glass,
I don't recall,
that is simply
the Dawn

and the shouts
disturb
the night
like shouts
like wild monody
with women's yells
certainly
accompanied by
a piano
a violin
or even
a flute

Vulture and Guard

Mykonos
Mycenae
fungus
three
words
yet
only two
wings
like stucco
like a woman
palm
shining
in the night
like a flesh-eating
violin

and perhaps
still
like glass
drills
inside
the thin
brains
of the poets

Is Alexander the Great Still Alive?

I burn my youth
that is a guitar
that is an artichoke
that is a kinnor

I mean the total
that is Merope
that is metope
that is ball

I cry for the memories
like a crow
like Quran
like a coral

I'm Minotaur
in the chest
under the sheet
inside the pearl

Event

In the middle of
Constantinople,
a bird sprouts the locals
call "magnolia"

The Clavichords of Silence

*Everything is silent, and silence is good only when
it hides joy inside it. Otherwise, I'm afraid of it.*

                                                    LE

the sperm
of wolfmen
burden
the stirring wheels
of the horizon
they throw
fiery flutes
under
the bloodied dresses
that hang
in the thick branches
of trees
they choke
the crows
in the mirrors
justice
and the compassion
of the kids

however,
I place red flowers
in her hair
I stand
erect
and naked
in the purple

gardens
and I vanish
in dark
caves
that hide
deep inside them
yellow fishes
that talk
like flowers

and perhaps
I'm that
wolfman
of the lightning
who, they say,
when evening comes
the man parenthesis
in the bellows
of the plot
in the shrouds
of the march
during
the night
when a bid
dies like a candle

thus, they fall
drop by drop
onto the temples
of the desperate
clavichords
the couples

of disappointed
and a heavy cloud
made of long
blonde hair
with brown eyes
it flies noiselessly
in long and narrow
basements
where harbours
and condors
bloom

and the silence
is fire
a rope ladder
they place carefully
on the lips
and a white
horse
that is a tree
close to the sea
and a red
horse
like
a flag

and I run
over the waters
tirelessly
with the lyrical
bicycle
with the helmet
of love

and when I arrive
at the last
step
of this dark
ladder
and I open
the door
of the room
I, then,
sense
that the room
was
is
big
garden
filled with music
and paintings

a room
full of bedsheets
thrown
in the garden

bedsheets
some fluttering
like flags
and like
windowpanes
and others were
thrown down
like mirrors
and others

38

spoke
inarticulate words
like chimneys
and others
spread
on beds
like comets
others looked
like jars
others were
like proboscis
and others
dressed
naked and beautiful
women
with dew
and tragic shouts

as is supposed to
perhaps I needed
to accept
the whole
situation
with a glass
that you put
on your eye
and see
a deep
water well
and in its depth
a b i r d

A Flute in the Yard of Hecatomb

The dead man *rushes* inside the dark dining room. For
someone to reach there, he must pass by an endless
line of chests filled with sealing wax. There, his hands
are filled with wreaths of colourful flowers, meant for
poets' heads. Besides, this is the *poetry of the forest*
with ambers and blind, moonlike flutes. The dead man
rushes and constantly counts: one, two, one, two/. His
whole effort is a tall wall, made of red bricks and with
the silent voice of a trumpet. Sometimes laughter is
heard or even a song, like a knife wound, or an ashtray.
Pointless, I then say, to saunter among the empty holes
of his eyes. At least, if my desperate shouts were matched
with joyous Aeolian harp! If one hysteria would sprout
on the edge of each of my fingers! Perhaps, it would be
possible to exile me deep, inside the musical oil lamps
with a heavy roll of fabric like a child's laughter. However,
nothing ... Everything is in vain. The dead man, alone,
rushes inside the dark dining room.

Umbrellas

for a while now
each night
comes regularly
and tyrannizes me
and crucifies me
and wounds me deeply
deathly
the word
banner
and I worry
being wild
and always ask
what this
might be again
and what
this strange
disturbance
means

is it perhaps
the message
of death and Joy
some gift
of goddess
Demetra or is it perhaps
what they call
crowbar (lotus) belt?

A thunderbolt
that fell

inside
a glass of milk

or perhaps
simply
the layered
tentacles
of a hippocampus
that sings
in the
morning, sunless parks
of the north
with the white
columns
the dust
of the statues
and the dead girl
we all loved
passionately
like a flower
and we named her
with the hurting
word
window
when we were young
very young
children?

Pomegranate Tree

listen to tears flowing
like motionless trees
silent
abandoned
when night falls

yet, the garden
I'm saying,
with the innumerable windows
was immense
and its greenery
reached down to the sea
where the yellow
sand starts
on this yellow
shore
I think,
we sang
our most beautiful songs

yet
they stoned us there
with handfuls
of stones
and pebbles

which were
the white
erotic teeth
of the women
we loved

Life and Death of the Poets

Sinope
is the name
the official name
of the Cloud-City
and City of Fires
which
is somewhere
in South America

this watery
and rather of Hellenic civilization
City
floats in the sky
like a baton
and the experts
place it,
sometimes in the middle
of a straight line
incised between Maracaibo
and Valparaiso
of Chile
other times
between Maracaibo
and Elbasan

there
as all the houses are made of fires
citizens live among the fires
they are constantly burned
and get reborn

from their ashes
exactly like
the bird
phoenix

exactly there
was born, as is known,
the great poet
of antiquity
Alector

during the excavations
among the ruins
they found
a strange poem
of that era
written on common paper
with steel
and bronze hooks
crisscrossed
and with the ink of tears

the poem was as follows:

come to the cypresses
to see the whirl of the diver

 because of the word
diver
in the beginning
the poem was seen as
dedicated to the great

Isidor Ducasse
who happened to come from
those
places

however, after serious thoughts
it was dedicated
irreversibly now
to a woman called
Beautiful Lady
known better by
her foreign name
Bella Donna

Voyage to Elbasan

I

Today I'll recall my impressions from travelling to Albania and remember that I need to announce that there is nothing simpler than a trip to that country. However, it is necessary, for anyone to understand that during the summer, the Saint John's celebration occurs. Only, when night falls, the nostalgia of old customs, makes everyone imagine that if they take part in the jumping of fires, they might be in any city they wish. I, once, during a day of utter loneliness, a day during which I had lived away from birds when night fell, I jumped over fires they had put on in one common neighbourhood of Athens and with a strong passion for Albania in my heart. I jumped once, twice. Nothing. The third time I suddenly found myself in Elbasan.

II

Elbasan is a big city that I can describe in detail, by talking about a song, in an unfamiliar language, of course, based on three notes that are repeated endlessly monotonically, always the same, from morning to evening, using a flute the blind man plays on the street corner. The side streets of Elbasan are extremely narrow and empty, gigantic walls stand on each side, walls that reach the sky. You don't see any little door anywhere, not even a tree branch that pokes through.

III

I saunter around this city with such curiosity. Serenity
reigned in my heart indeed I was singing between
my teeth, a song from my childhood.

    The men I met were very tall and wore long fousta-
nellas* down to the ground. Their walk was slow, graceful,
I'd say, as it is usually in the East. Some others wore caps on
their grey heads and others large, tragic women's hats with
feathers.

    However, suddenly, an inexplicable sadness covered
my heart. These people didn't have any eyes. I paid attention to them: their glances had already worried me. The
fear stopped me for a while and rendered me motionless
and silent. When I managed to stir somewhat and run
after them I finally realized that they'd vanish once
they reached the corner like a dream. They'd vanish to
reappear on the other corner from where they came to
continue their despicable saunter, unaffectedly.

    There was no doubt anymore. A horrible scam was
put together for me. I understood I was the victim of
a terrible trap. Then, as I realized the seriousness of
my mistake, I sat down and cried bitterly.

---

*   *Hellenic attire during the Ottoman Occupation Years*

The Mountains of Myopolis

I

the road
to love
is strewn with
eyes of cats
in the darkness
and silence
spreads around
like a net of joy

the road
to love
is nightly

it goes high
and reaches
where the blue
of cobalt
and the yellow
of cadmium
aren't anymore
the colours
I used to paint
my paintings
but tender music
of a harp
a kinnor
and sistrum
of escape

II

the foolish virgins
coupled
with the trees
in the forest
many virgins
and many trees
the time
of the great
rain

their uteruses were
untouched
pure
as much as after
as before the storm

yet
when the clouds vanished
and the sun
shone again
I remained
a prisoner
in the dark
living room
with the red velvets
and the heavy
persistent smell
of mould
and lust

through the window
I saw endless roofs
with marble railings
that went down
to the sea

and I was alone
with one
unfamiliar
man
leaning in darkness
over the piano keys
of the Clavichord of Silence

my face
was ravaged
like a leaper's
nothing was visible
from the regrets
and bitterness
of love

yet
the unfamiliar
man
every so often stood up
in his dark corner
and undisturbed
tyrannized me
from dawn
to darkness
and incised over
my forehead

like a terrible symbol
these words

father-mother

male-female

III

I decorate my forehead
with
fishes and umbrellas

I put in my hair
cries
of fire

my hands
become
the rusted
anchors
of shipwrecks
and while loneliness
is spread
slowly
on the seashore
I see the last lights
of death
vanish
over the sea
at the depth
of the horizon

Trap of the Castaways

I don't know what happens in the wild high mountains
at night or in the middle of the day. However, I know
all about the mysterious ghosts that live alone on peaks
of deserted hills. I know their habits well and that they
don't distance themselves from the high places they
have chosen as their residence. How the wanderer who
passes close by or from afar, noon hour or evening,
discerns them, sees them, sometimes fluttering like war
banners, other times taking strange shapes of four pieces
of wood under the cover of a thick layer of dry cypress
branches, like the tents Albanian shepherds put together
like the echo of a flute. Other times they travel on faraway
unexplored seas, on board ancient oil tanks, yet always,
under the Hellenic flag, certainly in memory of the god
Pan. Thus, the simple, natural, logical, and even psycholog-
ical result is to leave the factory lights on during the night
and the huge piles of garbage and empty cans in the fields.
Everything in the name of Pan. Yet, the electrical lights
Prove to be useless and only sometimes, here and there,
light wind-stricken seashores, wooden abandoned shacks,
seaweed and petrified bones of the flood animals and
marble busts of emperors and poets.

Concrete of Heroic Virgins

The timid virgins
get forgotten
when they fall
ah so early
fighting heroically
at the roadblocks

however, in the place
where their dead
head rolled
and their hair
was dragged
the poet likes
to isolate himself
in a pride
and light blue
loneliness

there
in this deserted
seashore
they put on fires
in the night
the lamps
that fool
the sailors

there, the thought
becomes
a fiery wheel

that rolls
on the horizon

there are
the islands that
turn into shrouds
when the wind
stirs crazily
the leaves
of palm trees

the buzz of the harbour
is located there
and piles of
dead seals
and spouts
of oil

there grow
trees
that produce
the strange and beautiful fruit
they offer
to the poet
for his future
bitterness

Psychoanalysis of Ghosts

If I don't have love, I sound
like bronze and tinkling cymbal
                                    St. Paul

When the ship of love enters the night, in the harbour,
the mysterious music of loneliness welcomes it. Around,
the waters are filled with flowers of every kind and
all colours and a line of naked women waits for us on
the quay. They are all ready, at our first signal, to put on
the red outfit of the divers. Not to dive into the bottom
of the sea but to come and wait for us, for long hours
tirelessly, tenderly, by the entrance of the subway. We,
of course, suddenly appear waving our big feathers and
yelling incoherent and beautiful words. Then, suddenly,
the quietness of the countryside turns more sensible
and men sprout out of the fields, men dressed in black,
who are comets and standing pianos with their white
keys that are the stars. Flags flutter in the wind,
machine guns are heard regularly, and children sing.
We hear the prophetic names of women we were meant
to love. The name of the city is Sinope too. However,
I'm not afraid of death because I love life.

Outcome

The dredger
of dreams
functions
with the addition
of words
oh, my proud dove
after,
of course,
the special permission
of the last
Alexandrian sculptor
and philosopher
of the first after Christian
years

however,
the outcome
is rather
pitiful
and condemnable
if we consider
all the works
of the sculptor
it is or not
half a dozen
toothbrushes

but when we consider
that all his philosophy
consists

of three bunches
of keys
hung
on three different
trees
between the lips
teeth
and breasts
of Hypatia

and when finally
we confess
that the dredger
doesn't truly
exist
and that
with this word
we meant
most likely
the chimneys
the autumnal wind
rips
over the roofs
of the houses.

They Passed the Forest

paper doves
flew inside
the dark colonnade
of the palace
and each flutter
of their wings
ςασ
the deep glance
of the Kore was too
like the fall
of a stone
in the sea
or
the promise
of a distant
joy

lower
the thin dresses
with the colourful flowers
that the wind caressed
and were worn
by wooden
statues
with still wooden eyes
and clay
hair

wooden statues
named

Maria
named
bottle
tallow
bicycle
named
spark

Hydra

he was accused
of being extra dangerous
for the public
safety
for the peace
of peaceful citizens
when
the serious
or rather looking serious
priests
rather aged
and respectful
or not
they invoked
the memory
of the great naval battles
of Salamis
and the memory
of Miaoulis, Kanaris, Tobazis,
Lazarus Kountouriotis,
and Isidor Ducasse

they arrested him
at dawn
they tied his hands behind his back
and lifting him
like a corpse
to a skinny
white virgin
named Maria

a lace
of exquisite beauty,
lace like my paintings,
under the shadow
of the mountain
and the green
garden

they threw him,
women told me,
in the middle
of red flowers
and red velvety
partitions
by palm trees-windows
and old furniture
however, clean
with the lamp
the glass of the lamp
since it was,
women told me,
Saturday evening
toward Sunday dawn

Saturday night
Sunday dawn

the sea was visible
through the door
a part of the sea,
light blue,
the stairs climbed up

and I called my heart
sorrowfully
in regular
or irregular times
Hector
Hector of horses

while Hecuba
in this case
was the huge
terrible shadow
of my brain

Morning Song

once
I asked why
the tragic
and timid virgin
called Pulcheria,
the day before
her wedding
was mopping carefully
the whole house
and she died
next day?

Since
she cleaned and tidied
everything
why didn't she
enjoyed
the long white
lace
the exquisite white frills
and the colourful
huge wedding
feathers?

Why
she silently placed
the big yellow butterfly
and the paper flowers
that were inside
her head

on the planks?
And the stuffed
caged bird
of her breasts?
Why?

Because,
my father perhaps said,
the soldier must have
his cigarette
the baby
his cradle
and the poet
his mushrooms

because
the soldier must have
his plot
the young boy
his grave
and the poet
his rattle

because
the soldier must have
his adze
the young boy
his glace
and the poet
his plane

On Lyrical Chimneys

To the memory of the great poets
Alexander Antoniou and Kyriazis Kalfoglou

The nightmare couldn't be explained although the day had
progressed fast and the afternoon golden-yellow hours
had arrived. Let us admit the whole drama was laid on
the French word chimney sweeper. This word fit him and
suddenly threw him into the depths of sadness and joy
raised him to the highest tops of trees, and pushed him
onto the desertedlandscape of the moon, strewn with
mirrors and beautifuland decorative musical albums.
He, then, leaned down serenelyand raised her precious
dresses to kiss her long, white hands. She, then, went to the
window, and her head, a red electric lamp, was constantly
lit and turned off during the night. This was enough for
the announcement of the shipwreck to the ends of the
Earth and the loss and the rising to the heavens of the
muzzle-loading, paper-dynamite-moved, smuggling ship
"Pleias". As soon as the pleasant news arrived, the name
and route of floating rivers were changed and women
devoted themselves to the strange, lustful caresses of birds,
and others, naked, went out to the streets, from the vacant
fabric factories when night fell. Let us not forget that flutes
were playing the song of the drawer during the unfolding
of the drama, which song Nikos Engonopoulos from
Constantinople will explain in his future collected poems
edition.

When Midnight Comes,
Jef, the Great Automaton …

Est-ce quelque dedale ou ta raison perdue
ne se retrouve pas?

Fr. De Malherbe

When midnight comes, Jef, the great automaton proudly
says the words, eternal words and deceptive and futile, yet
so advantageous for the satin eyes we loved, remember? Do
you remember or would you rather try to tame them into
a siren's voice in the nets of their hair, which mercilessly
ploughed the knitted and turned-off lamps of the flowing
water…the flowing voices…the imagination…of the great
erotic beds. Nothing of all these? Nothing. Then, the
heights are meant for us. We must focus on the heights.
Like the nihilist, who sprouts up in the air like a live flower.
And as we must come down from the heights, let us do so.
But, then again, with flowers, like flowers, with palaces,
with spring music, with words of love and eyes of love.
Set aside, be joyous, with your big eyebrows and open
the big eyelids of the cloud. Look: the metal flutes are in a
straight line over the carpet of dew. Here is what we call
joy. Yes, this is known as *the tender touch of a beloved woman.*
This is *the law of life, the frontman of the sun, the sun of silence.*
Pay attention to these words. They have many obvious and
hidden meanings. They are words full of metaphysical
concepts, they are the depths of bitterness and mountains
of joy. They are words life says, words the noisy piano key
of love says, the bronze echo of love, Jef, the midnight great
automaton.

Exactly Like

Ta memoire pareille aux fables incertaines
                              Ch. Baudelaire

CHORUS:
what were you
looking for
alone
on that
narrow-long balcony
with the long black lace
in the night?

What were you
looking for
when you threw
down to the road
many flowers
and all the joy of a night?

What were you
looking for
when you sauntered alone,
wearing
the sky dress,
in the night
among the kaleidoscopes
and during the day
among the machines?

Are you the sun,

the fish
the craft-mast
the tree
or Pharao Nectanebo?

POET:
No

I am the one who saw
the architect
and the mother
the poet and the mother
I looked for
joy
the seed
of the night
the violin of sleep
the ash

CHORUS:
Yet

tell us
what did you find?

POET:

In the forest
with the low cypresses

I found

the wooden
figure
of the ship
with her blond hair
fluttering
in the wind

it has lines
of necklaces
made of shining stars
around
her neck
....
in the night
when tears
scar my face
like a river
that flows
from my eyes

now
when I wake up
I look at her
next to me
gleaming
with her belly
like a flashlight

To the Friends of Cities

solemn horse rides
lean over fresh pools
with oleanders
their steps echo in the night enigmatically
over the cobblestones
their only purpose is
their fastest possible
group arrest
of the most faraway seafarers
and their fast
incarceration
inside steel chests

because it's thought that
and they have truly been
the reasons
of the early waste
of forest damaging
avalanches
since only
this way
the smooth function
of bicycle races
is secured
because
only this way
they can guard
the full of dust
ring
of fungi

like the birds in the sky
the flowers of virgins

however,
do they fully
agree with
the adopting
the above measures
and caring, I'd say,
bad omened radio operators
of earthly
ships?

I don't know

the wooden statues
have the right to talk
and the infections
and the etesian winds
of misfortune
the right to talk belongs
to the horses
of virgins
the nocturnal optimistic
announcements
the unexplored sea of life

and now the Pasiphae drama
is unfolding

Bolivar

A Hellenic Poem

1944

For the great, the free, the brave, the strong
great words, and free, and courageous and
                        strong suit them
for those are the absolute submission of each
element, the silence, tears, and lighthouses are
for them, and olive branches, and lampposts
which jump at the rocking of ships and write
            on the dark horizons of harbours
for those are the empty barrels that were piled
            in the narrowest side street of the harbour
for those are the coiled white ropes, the chains,
                    the anchors and the manometers
in the irritating smell of petroleum
to arm the ship and sail away, to leave
like the tram that starts, empty and fully lit
            in the night serenity of the gardens
with the destination: to the stars.

For those, I'll speak the beautiful words, that
                    inspiration recited to me
as in the depths of my mind, the emotion nested
for the austere and beautiful faces of Odysseus
                Androutsos and Simon Bolivar.
However, for now, I shall sing only of Simon, I leave
                the other for a suitable time
so that I shall sing for him the most beautiful song
                that I ever sang
perhaps the most beautiful song that I ever sang in
                the world.
And these not because they both stood for their lands

and nations and borders and other similar things that
                    don't inspire
but because they both always stood alone, free, great,
                    brave and strong throughout the eons.

And now, I despair that even today no one ever
understood me, but what am I saying, nobody wished
                    to understand me.
Certainly, the same luck might be applied to the words
about Bolivar which I'll repeat tomorrow about
                    Androutsos?
Besides, it isn't easy, to sense the importance of faces
                    such as Androutsos and Bolivar
Similar symbols.
But let us pass quickly: no, in the name of God, not
         any emotions, exaggerations and despairs.
Indifferent, my voice was meant for the eons.
(In the near or distant future, in a few or many years,
perhaps the day after tomorrow or the day after that,
until the hour when the Earth will start flowing empty,
useless and dead in space, new people will wake up,
with mathematical accuracy, during the wild nights,
on their beds, they might shed tears on their pillows
and wondered who I was, thinking that I existed once,
                    what words I said, and hymns I sang.
And the huge waves that each evening splash onto
                    the seven shores of Hydra
and the wild rocks and the high mountain from which
                    the storm charges down
endlessly, tirelessly, they shall call my name).

However, let us return to Simon Bolivar.

Bolivar! Name made of steel and wood, you were
                    a flower in the gardens
                            of South America.
You had the kindness of all flowers in your heart,
                              in your hair,
                              in your glance.
Your hand was big like your heart and spread
                            both good and evil.
You rolled down the mountains and the stars
shivered, you descended to the plains with the golden
                    epaulets all the insignia of your rank
with the rifle resting on your shoulder, with your bare
                        chest, with your body
                        full of wounds
and naked you sat on the low rock by the shore and
they came and painted you with the symbols of
                            Indian warriors
with whitewash, half white, half light blue to be like
a humble temple by the shores of Attica, like a church
in the Tatavla neighbourhood, like a palace in
                        a deserted Macedonian city.

Bolivar! You were reality, and you are now, you aren't
                        a dream.
When the wild hunters nail the wild eagles and other
wild birds and animals onto the wooden doors
                        of the forests
you are reborn, and you shout, and you are hit, and
        you are the hammer, the nail and the eagle.

If winds blow over the coral islands and turn upside
the lonely caiques,
and parrots go wild with their voices when the day
ends and the gardens get serene drowned in humidity
and crows perch on the tall trees,
think, near the waves, the metal tables of the café
how in the darkness the wind ravages them and
faraway
the light is turned on and off, turns around and
then dawn comes, how terrible agony, after a night
without sleep
and the water discloses none of its secrets.
That's life
and the sun rises, and the houses by the quay, with
the island rooms,
painted rosy and green, with white ledges (Naxos
and Chios)
This is
Bolivar!

Bolivar! I cry out your name, lying on the top of
Mount Ere, the highest peak on Hydra Island.
From here the view majestically extends up to
the Saronic islands, to Thebes, all the way
to Monemvasia, the great Egypt,
and to Panama, Guatemala, Nicaragua, Honduras,
Haiti, San Domingo, Bolivia, Columbia, Perou,
Venezuela, Chile, Argentina, Brazil, Paraguay,
Ecuador, even to Mexico.
With a hardened lithos, I incise your name in
stone, so that people may come and pay
their respects.

Sparkles fly up as I incise, such was Bolivar,
they say,
and I observe my hand as it writes in the bright
sun.
You saw the light for the first time in Caracas.
Your light, oh Bolivar, since before you were born
South America was covered by bitter darkness.
Now your name is a lighted torch that lights
America, the North and the South, and the whole
World.
The rivers Amazon and Orinoco, spring out of
your eyes.
The high mountains are rooted in your breast.
The Andes Mountain range is your spine.
On top of your head, brave man, run the wild
horses and wild cattle.
The wealth of Argentina.
The endless coffee plantations spread onto
your belly.

When you talk, terrible earthquakes ravage
the lands
from the imposing deserts of Patagonia to the
colourful islands
volcanos erupt in Peru and exhume their anger
to the skies
the earth trembles and the icons creak in Kastoria.
In the silent city close to the lake.
Bolivar, you are beautiful like a Hellene.

As a child, I first met you on an uphill Phanari
                                side street.
A hanging lamp in the Byzantine Temple lit
                                your kind face.
Were you, I wonder, one of the myriad faces

that Constantine Palaiologos assumed and left
                                behind?

Boyaca, Ayacucho, bright and eternal concepts.
                                I was there.
We had passed through there to the old borders.
Far behind, they had started the fires in Leskovik.
During the night, the army climbed up toward
                                the battle
from where familiar sounds were heard. Next to
it, going down, endless busses carried
                                the wounded.

Don't let anyone get disturbed. Down there is
                                the lake.
They'll pass through here, behind the cane fields.
The roads were compromised: work and glory to
Hormovitis, who is famous for such things.
The whistle is heard. To your positions, march!
Come, dismount the horses. Put the cannons
in their positions, get a towel, clean the bores,
light fuses, hold them tight.
The cannon balls are to the right. Vras!
Vras, fire, in Albanian: Bolivar!

Each hand grenade thrown and blown
was a rose for the glory of the great general
tough, undisturbed as he stood amid the dust
                              and the destruction
glancing at the endlessness, his forehead
                              toward the clouds
and his image was a terrible spring of awe, a path
                    to justice, the gate of salvation.
However, so many conspired against you, Bolivar,
so many traps they set so that you could fall into
especially one snake, a man from Philipoupolis
but nothing stirred you as you stood an unshaken
tower in front of the Aconcagua terror, holding
a terrible club and brandished it over your head.
The bald condors were scared although the battle's
fear and thick smoke never scared them before and
                         they flew away in big groups.
And the female lamas ran down the slopes
Creating avalanches of stones, rocks, and soil.
And your enemies vanished down to Tartarus
                    where they hid
(When the best marble from Alabandus will arrive
I'll spring my forehead with the blessed water
of Vlachernes, I shall apply all my craftiness
to chisel that image of you and place it like a new
Kouros on the mountains of Sikinos, and never forget
to write the famous *Greetings oh passerby*
                    on the pedestal.

And here we must admit that Bolivar never feared, or
hesitated in front of any battle, in front of the most

dreadful, as they call it, the moment of the inescapable
                    bitter blackness of treason.
They say he knew from the beginning, with unimaginable
accuracy, the day, the hour, even the second: the moment
of the great battle that was fought for him alone, in
which he was not only the army but the enemy too,
                    the victor and defeated too
triumphant hero and expiatory victim too.

(And the beautiful pneuma of Cyril Lucaris dwelled
                    inside of him
how he serenely fooled the horrible trap of the Jesuits
and of that man from Philpoupolis)

And if he was lost, if a Bolivar ever gets lost, who was
                    risen to the sky like Apollo's sun,
gleaming he went down, in unimaginable glory, behind
the polite mountains of Attica and Morias.

Invocation

Bolivar, you are the son of Rigas Feraios, and of Antony
Economou, so unjustly slaughtered, and a brother
                    of Patsatzoglou,
The dream of the great Maximilian de Robespierre is
reborn
                    upon your forehead.
You are the liberator of South America.
I don't know which relation connected you if the other
great
American from Montevideo, was your descendant, one is
surely known, that I am your son.

Chorus

Strophe
(Entrance of guitars)

As the night is slow in passing
it sends the old moons to console us
as ghosts of darkness load lissome virgins with
loosened hair onto the plains
the time of victory has come, the time of triumph.
The empty shells of warmonger generals will be
dressed in bloodied-cocked hats
and the red colour they had before the sacrifice
will cover with shine the fluttering flags.

Antistrophe
(the love of liberty brought us here)

ploughs by the roots of palm trees
and the sun
that rises gleaming
over the trophies
and birds
and spears
will announce up to where the tear flows
and the wind takes it
to the sea's
depths
the horrible oath
the most horrible darkness
the terrible fable:
Libertad

Epode
(chorus of Freemasons)

Go away curses, don't come close,
                    Corazon
from cradles to the stars, from the womb to the eyes,
                    Corazon
where sharp rocks and volcanos and seals
                    Corazon
where a dark face with big lips and white teeth
                    Corazon
let the phallus stand let the celebration start with
human sacrifices and dance
                    Corazon
amid the revel of the flesh to the glory of ancestors
                    Corazon
so that they shall sow the new generation
                    Corazon

Conclusion

After the success of the South American Revolution,
a bronze statue of Bolivar was erected in Nafplion and
Monemvasia, on a deserted hill overlooking the city.
However, since the overcoat of the hero was stirred
by the strong wind, the resulting noise was so great
that it made it impossible for people to sleep. Thus,
the citizens demanded and managed to tear down
the monument.

Farewell Hymn to Bolivar

(Distant music is heard here, playing in utmost sadness
nostalgic folk songs and dances of South America,
preferably in Sardana rhythm)

general
what were you doing in Larissa
you, a man from Hydra?

Return of the Birds

1946

Forth from the war emerging, a book I have made,
The words of my book nothing, the drift of it
      everything,
A book separate, not link'd with the rest nor felt
      by the intellect
But you ye untold latencies will thrill to every
      page

Walt Whitman

Voices

For Andre Breton

through the shut blinds
during the yellow fire
of noon
when the statues are silent
and the myths agree
voices
vibrate
in the side street
slowly
at first
then thundering
in a fast pace
and they suddenly reveal
the eternal secrets

other times,
certainly,
they are terrible and scary
like tombs
and other times
like the caress
of long
fine
fingers

and call each
with their name

they call
the spring water
mouth
the tall,
black trees
forgetfulness
the night
in the ravines
Omphale

they call the crying eyes
girlfriend
the fresh red lips
leaves
the erotic teeth
nightmare

the purple bedsheets of Eros
abysses
the black waters
of the harbour
oil lamp
and they call
the rusted anchors
the lament
of dream

they put colourful feathers
on the saddened
glance of Orpheus
on Orpheus' hands
they place fans

they rip
his flamed
cloths
they decorate his head
with fine lace

(They secure
flags
onto Orpheus's
head)

they spread
blood
on the chaos of oracles
and they call
the palm trees
torches
again

they stay
sobbing
on the word hammer
they call silence
the word gate
they call death
music
between the temples
and they call
my heart
a forest
in the night

Esthetic and Graceful Dance

The great poet Kafoglou wasn't only a beautiful teacher of
logos and dreams that we know. He was, and this is one
of the many dark and secret facets of the poets, a great
and exceptional musician. Certainly, and always in his
imaginary rhythm of flowers. He was the one, before
any other, who used the piano as a wind instrument.
To perform a certain piece, the hardest, in this way, he
disguised himself first like a marble statue which they
erected, preferably, in a desert or an abandoned garden.
Then, as soon as the red colours of the dusk started
spreading in the sky, they carefully dug a hideout in the
back of the statue, into which a boy could hide and talk as
if the statue did the talking. Then, the dead poet grabbed a
hammer in his strong hands and hit the piano with extra
force so pieces scattered around. The metal hulls of ships
started moaning at once. Sheet metal echoed in the air
as the strong wind carried them over the roofs of storage
rooms. The terrible wrath of the Lord swept everything
away: the proud, high palaces with their many rooms
up to the humble shack of the worker. And only lace fell
every half hour and covered the hot nakedness of the
beautiful women. Lovers committed suicide each morning.
Fountains rose from where there were two words written
"Special name" or even "in the name" or "impossible to
escape". One night, in the middle of Boeotia, all the lamps
were turned off as the sea washed them away. When the
poet, on top of his lyrical crescendo, put down the big
hammer slowly, soft serenity spread over the world and
green shining ostracons adorned his long golden braids.
The piano had performed its duty and automatically

transformed itself into a line of copper candlesticks
or white and rosy doric columns and a long line of sad
women's eyes, beautiful and each pair of a different
colour. There is no need to add and out of respect and the
restitution of truth, that the great poet Kalfoglou is just
an excuse, a simple excuse. Since the poet, the statue, the
young boy and the gallows I mentioned were not but I, only
I, perhaps in the old, or current, indeed the most current
times.

The Gods are Jealous

Lord, how painful, terrible, big problem! Are
the Gods jealous? I mean, not whether the Gods
are jealous or not, but whether the Gods are jealous
or jealous!

The Soldier's Song

the black wind
starts crazily
from its dark
hideouts
it roars
like a beast
passing deserted
narrow side streets
and charges
through
the unhinged doors
that don't
lock anymore
the sharp
nails
of my lust
it charges unbearably
through
the wooden
abandoned stairs
that constantly cry
with human voices
like an Aeolian harp
it roars
in the gigantic
dead rooms
it whistles
going through
chimneys

and cracks
of the ceiling

after it carries along
the smoke of wood
that secretly burn
somewhere
among the grassy
empty
yards

and reappears
high up
in the sky
and dishevels
the black clouds

it stirs
changes
in the immenseness
their silent
threats
and goes down again
swiftly
toward
the edge
of the lake

and its terrible
charge comes
and breaks
and scatters

like a victorious
resistance
against
the white
thin and tall
poplars
with a myriad
voices
into the black
saddened
silent
poplars

and the black lake
recalls,
undisturbed
with its black
hanging
waters,
the black
legends
its shores
black and
sharp
the deserted
mosques
the tumbled
army barracks
the ploughs
the rocks
the white
harmonious

women
with the dark
glance of begging

that I
uprooted
from their eyes
like in a similar
time when
I was once tossed
about
in the rough seas
against the wind
down there
toward
the land
of Monemvasia

Gothic Bitterness

For Andreas Embirikos

The spring waters of Epirus with its brave men are
enough. The sperm collectors with their books are
enough. The devious penetrations of underwater gongs
into the atmospheric layers of forgetfulness are enough.
They are enough. Now, our souls need serenity. Now
our souls yearn for joy. Even if we need, momentarily,
one more time, for one future moment or yesterday's
to write the ex-vitro pregnancy of fear onto the logs
of immortality, even if it is necessary to abandon the
quarries inside the diving suits, to place birds into
geometric shapes on top of the embrasures or to place
the lookout of aura onto the aphrodisiacal nakedness
of the forest. Even if the sacrifice demanded of us was
so painful as the tears flowing from her sad eyes or
the tragic braids of her hair. Even if our move to the
faraway Ecbatana hides many current and future
horrible results. Here are, the humble slander, the
venerable fig eater who just flowered on the warring
candelabras. Chalcedon was silent, indeed. Her song
is repeated now by the waters in an ashy rhythm. Is
this flag yours? Is this blood yours? Are these swords
yours? Does the chaos of a dream suit infinity? Where is
this defence taking us when even the osier hates us?

Return of Euridice

in the little
harbour
touched by
the tears
of fishes
like the last
drops
of the sun
life rises
and sits quietly
on marble basins
and bitter
lotus flowers
along with
the nostalgic
rhythms
of bassoons
and the night

and look
the time has come
the dreams
are reborn
as were told
to childhood agates
the palm trees got crazy
and fiery
they rose
their white
hands

to the stars
and the moans
of lust
to darkness

and now
messages
grabbed
the banners
that fluttered
in the unconquerable
hideouts
of the wild
forests
and the tender
voices
are heard again
coming
from
the depths
of the lit
horizons

and the sobs
painted by
the empty glances
of fever
the tambourines
on the reverent
branches
slowly
go silent

since the cry
of separation
will be soon
forgotten

when the beast
appears
wind-whipped
like a log
in the wind-whirl
 of jealousy
not the familiar
Minotaur
but a bull
with a man's head

and behind
the wide
wings
flutter
like a beast's
that roared
on statues'
pedestals
and oil lamps
that point
to the road
with torches
leading
the procession

followed by

untouched
virgins
who committed
an indecent act
on salvation's
antiphons
and buckles
on shrouds
they come
and with their hands
pointing to
the tree
of life
and death

however
they don't fool me
because
my lips
are mercilessly ravaged
by the avenge
and by the pelican
of sacrifice
and because
in my eyes
the horrible
thunderbolts
of the sea
spread roots

and if
the profane cycle

didn't manage
to live
inside
my essence
the flesh-eating
ships
and my proud
wind shouts
woke up
the terrible
deserts
the night
embraces

and if the procession
flows
on the road
under the light
of the torches
and the sistrum
and always
the bull
upfront
man-like
and the last
virgins
in black clothes

however
I know it:
I'm
the only man

who sheds tears
when these lyrical
sacrificial
lambs
passed
and I know
that the imaginary
tree
is the only tree
of life

it's
the tree
that holds
the eternal secret
of forgetfulness
in its palms

and it's
the tree
that always
and patiently
I expected
to become
one with
its foliage

it's
the only tree
with flowers
that always
sang

the song
of my joy

and it's Euridice

Euridice
who comes
and leaves
and R E T U R N S
to stay
finally
amid
the horrible
wound
of my wild
viscera

and perhaps
to prove
the old oracle
that claimed
that
I'm Orpheus
the tall
light
and immortal
born from
the wide
breasts
of Hermes
the Trismegistus

and now
that the dream
triumphed
in the small harbour
into which
the fire of
the palm trees
moored
and in the marble
basins
the joy of the sun
is spread over
only
the bassoons
sing
when
the night falls

Dyadic Automation

Careful! Cover yourselves! Be careful! The blowing winds have already brought the mysterious messages to our ears. Everything around us is just another threat. There wasn't any neighbourhood not blanketed by fear, each object hides a soul inside it. Come, let's go. The time is now. The rusty weathercock calls us wildly in the night. The draw-well stopped and the blind horses became one with the begonia flowers. Let's go, march! To go far away to Galvana. The saviour plank is hidden from the wind harbour of forgetfulness, peace is there. Sacrificial victims of love, ascetic wanderers of the night, proud dawn walkers light up the sea lamp. Whoever has the strength, whose heart truly dares, let him come. But let us not delay in futile reviews of the past. The time is uncertain. The roads aren't safe at all and the flood drenched many places. The Caryatid girls have crowded erotically the dark ditches, the lustful maidens of our erotic years. Their famous smile flew away and now it blooms in some abandoned islands. The thunderbolt shows us the way. Let's go! To the Lycaonian Galvana, there we shall rest. After our kind foreheads are decorated with rose flowers, we offer the libations due to the birds. There, in the graceful wooden temples of the old capital, we shall slaughter the young bull and a fiery column will spring out from its shed blood. There, wrapped around phallic banners, girls are more beautiful than sudden conclusions of dynamite. There lives the Hellene Pantelas among the wild Soudanese. The flowers there are wise and sunlit leftovers of dead beauties. The tears of the shark and the enigmatic prayer of Zacharia are useless there along with the frosty embrace of the penguin.

The erotic spasms of the last emperors and their fiery tears belong to the same person. The offer of the boatswain to the footprints of the hypotenuse of anomalous attractions is accompanied by the angelic harp, and our imposing stature means the spread of freedom and the longing for freedom all over the globe.

Master of Karytaina

The Master of Karytaina, that famous man...
Chronicle of Morea

Who is he who raised a warring staff and walked
the whole night and he dwelled in bogs
who decorated his forehead with celery and myrtle
and covered his nakedness with lyrical overcoats?

Who is he that in the foggy noon of sadness
he fought against the world and was victorious
who dragged blonde braids over the plains and
filled moats and crevasses with the brightest eyes?

Who is he, who in his chest, relived the myth of life
and of the dream, myth of the mind and the body
who was like a ship that left and never to return
who was a statue standing by abandoned shores?

Who during the sun's descent behind mountains
shone fully flooded like a spotted eagle
who is the pride of the day and the shield of dawn
the night's worthy lover in the secretive alcove?

If he's the man, the thirteen nymphs fell in love with
before any other let him go and drink the immortality
water
and if he is the saviour and the icon lover
before he speaks, let his shadow dissolve and vanish.

For eons, they waited for him in the deserted houses
in the dark mirrors and the closed windows
hearts ploughed by the pain of love
eyes gruesomely furrowed by the lustful longing

and as soon as he comes, he will raise his axe
to feed the rivers and the heroic fire with blood
the viscera he uprooted he will sow into the winds
and he will take his revenge in the Castle of Silence.

Greetings

the regrets of the world of beloved women
in many cities
seem like motherhood in films
and the enigmatic locales
while on the asphalt,
try to remember,
what a wail
what buildings
what precessions
to give us
to save us

yet inside the black eyes
the fleeting life
exists
and lives and persists
in the black eyes
filled with
yellow
roses
with all
the deep fear
of spring

don't sing:
to the white legs
to reverent lips
of drunkenness

with flowers
of the fields

we wandered over the earth,
lost child,
what a tiredness
so many tears
we survived the day before
the holidays
tender and sad
thyme
prayer
west

black firstborn
crests
hills
always Eleonor always
the pistol was enough
to the questions of the temples
please show us
your heart
your mind
and we shall tell you

ethereal poets
gesticulate
in the evening
you seek
to always find
here are the temples
and graves

and arches
of triumph

L' amour l'oulbli
the trees the trees the trees
rain
read
your grief in the clouds

what do
the gardens say
they feel too
or else
with boredom

I never met
myself
I hear voices
sea winds
beyond that birch forest
the small
cove
is the whole story

wait:
returning from the fields
in the afternoon
in the rain

we found
the adventures of nostalgia

Joyless Poem Dedicated to a Beautiful Woman Provider of Lust and Serenity

since you want it
beautiful and harmonious woman
one night in May, you placed modestly and politely
a white gardenia
among the dead flowers
inside the old, Italian I believe, vase with
light blue depictions of monsters and chimeras
come
fall in my arms
and gift me,
since you want it,
the sadness of your green glance
the deep bitterness of your red lips
the mystery of night knit among your long hair
and the embers of your exquisite body

Fellow Traveller in Melancholy

As she realized how much my tragic love for her overtook my heart, she invited me, among the ruins of the London Tower, for a cup of tea from the same hands, named by the killers of her lovers, depending on the season, sometimes "shovels", other times "shiners". She accompanied her offer with the only word she had kept inside her for years like something precious, she said, more than her life, like a secret gift of her breasts in the tempest of my lust. I raised my eyes and looked, as an unexpected shiver shook my body: she was naked before the year's fountain, the fans of a nighty fire sprouted out of her belly and the wall was splattered with blood. I felt that the famous, "better tomorrow" had arrived, was a present reality. It was obvious that everything from the past was already erased, the nightmare of the tropics and the harbour had already vanished. I was a gigantic red eagle that saw, from a young age, the closing eyes of the opposite sun. She was the big, dark forest spread among the chandeliers, the chest and the big hallway mirror used for official palace events. Her thought was crown, her glance renaissance, her glance a beak. Her name was Rodamne. She had lived in faraway lands from where she had come to meet me. I told her I freaked out, thinking we hadn't met earlier. How could she have, via the measure of the beautiful woman she was, replaced her eyes with two green Egyptian scarabs and she didn't see me when I passed her? She had probably cut her long hair short so that the words that escaped from my mouth were one cathedral church built, for the only purpose of executing at the site and a specific moment, the unknown archbishop, and seller of small items, from an irregular Mexican squad. She didn't talk, she didn't stir, she only took in her embrace the flowers that decorated the room and scattered them in the fresh ravines, in orchards with the delayed hunter, at the foothills of the Memories Mountains. The candles burned joyously on the graceful bronze candelabras and the song she sang teary-eyed had the same meaning with the phrase "time for Shaba" in the Hebrew neighbourhoods of Thessaly cities.

Theano

The great initiates
with the hot,
beautiful bodies
under
the linen dresses
with the harmonious
pleats
appeared before me
at the window of a Parisian café
and signalled to me
to meet them
outside

the cobblestone road shone after the night
rain
and reflected lights
and bright shapes
and car headlights

I forgot to mention
this scene unfolded in Constantinople
somewhere close to the Dry Fountain
near the Old Walls
indeed, it happened that night
the local movie theatre
was showing
the famous film
Pax tibi Marce Evangelista meus

Early Matins

what created a stir in me
and captivated
the people
was my exact
likeness
to Abraham Lincoln

indeed, when my bronze statue
was erected
in one square of Piraeus
they laid
by my feet
something,
I couldn't discern
from the top of the pedestal,
that looked like
a corpse
like a copper
stove
with burning charcoal

I waited until night came
and when I went near
to see
I discovered
with such joy

it wasn't anything else
but
the black eyes
of the woman I love
that gleamed in
the darkness

Dumont D'Urville

a black woman sits by the roots
of a palm tree for the whole day
she has two red carnations in her eyes
and she has two fish under her arms
one of them light blue
the other dark red
and she has an acacia between her breasts
and she has an acacia between her legs
a palm tree all day long

Gardens in the High Noon

The white body of the woman
was lit
from within
with such a bright light
that
I had to
take the lamp
and put it
on the floor
so that
the shadows
of our tender bodies
could be projected
on the wall
with a biblical religiosity

the lamp shone constantly
during the whole night,
the source of oil was inexhaustible,
the following day
and the next one
onto the floor
the rich piled
carpets
the beautiful fruit
the brightest flowers

with white and red
oleanders reigned everywhere

the atmosphere was symbolic,
from a yellow: a golden yellow.

Hydra of the Birds

Long-lasting music concerts, opaline sparkles of our first
       house in the heat of summer
in the endless quest at the Tiera del Fuego, on plains,
       forests, skies
I'll softly kiss the lips of the icon; with hope, I'll grace
       conches and castles
that silently stand by what the Muses touch and when
       skylights go down behind the cypresses
they plow caresses of undergrowth with wooden horses
reverent caresses of secret dinosaurs, by the nets of
       waters that swans have encircled
black swans, light blue, full of ideas and lust meant to
       vanish and abruptly seeks
to climb higher, to tumble, to destroy, to open windows,
       to cry, so I'll shout
I'll ravage, it will moor, get ripped, I'll mark in copper
       deeper, deeper
doves, lions, her night hair, the soldier's weapon, the
       Albanian soil
and to where it might reach, the imagination of the metal,
       words Pythia said in her dry extensions,
Tropics and wells it'll pass until playful dawn comes
       with the debauchery of the fleshless Kurds
to buy guitars that choke my eyes until I pull the peplums
       held by moon
to tie my face to the shape of a bird.

Picasso

For Pablo Picasso

The matador after all lives in Ellassona
by the cobblestone square under the plane trees
and the café owner goes back and forth refilling
his cup of coffee and the smoke of his narghile
while the hours of the day
pass nostalgically
and myriads of birds gather
in the branches of the plane trees
that means sundown is upon them

then the plotters slip out of the side street
the night falls silently and helps them
to gather like the birds, but unseen
and where they want
while heavy tears drip down their crafty eyes

and the mother, who wants to stop the fascists
inside the dark room where the plotters discuss things
and peppers dry up hanging from the ceiling,
with her knotty hands adorned with rings,
takes off the glass of the lamp and lights it
then she quietly wipes with her apron
her knotty hands dirtied by the oil

and as we said she wants to stop the killers
the old woman takes the lamp from the table
and opens the window in a rush

and, in the night, she extends the lit lamp
out of the window

old mother, they tell her
where are you taking the lamp?
However, no suspicious shadows with
machine gun underarms moved in fields of Avila
and seen from afar, the light outside
of the window shone like a star
and guitars were heard echoing slowly

and the gypsy girls started their dance.
Girls with wide pelvis and fluttering
colourful loosened dresses
while from their hot, and crayoned lips
wild cries of pain were heard
like words of a song: "I'll tell you
about my loneliness with Soleares"

and the major guitars went frenetic
and the fascist murderers were shooting at the crowd
and they tramped my heart
with their satin high-heeled shoes
striking the cobblestone road

then something happens to make you lose your mind
when a red-haired bull jumped in the middle
flames fired up from his nostrils and
the banderillas painfully poked his shoulder
        and back
and he started butting here and there
        to gore

to deeply pierce the flesh with his horns
and toss up in the air each person
        he butted
and a mountain of bodies were piled
bodies of men and horses
in rivers of blood

(banderillas painfully decorated his neck and back)

and the girls with the beautiful breasts lay down
        on their backs
and suns went down and rose again,
in their beautiful eyes

Let us Say ...

Captains of trawlers pulled the gigantic beast out to the shore. It writhed on the sand with its soft white belly to the sun. The air smelled like rotting flesh while the animal stirred its wide slippery legs. People gathered around to study the horrible sight of the beast, to follow its slow agony. I too wanted to go close to see but it was impossible due to the big crowd. One lady, dressed only in her hat, loaded with enigmatic feathers whispered to me tenderly: "It is blind" Ah, so it is! But since it is blind what was the reason Seurat told us about the red crown around the green foliage along the Parisian avenues when the lights were turned on? What is the noise of children's voices that the trolley bus doesn't let us hear clearly? Why have you put on these velvet gloves today? Don't take off your shoes, the night is expected to be peaceful. Then night fell. The beast was forgotten, the captains of trawlers had left, and the crowd was gone. The moon was made of tin and they carried it onto the space with a string. The curtain started to close.

Vulture 1748

(painter's explanation)

The right or wrong longing drove
the twilight
of the young peltast
to the unstopped nocturnal mountains
into the wild crevasses of Orthodoxy
into the thick glens and cypresses of panic
to the moral promotion
of the tough Fate along
colonnades of morning matins and torpor?

Who could be the leader
of rebellion
fame
love
rhetor?

They have been true to who's bidding
but the petty officers?
Father killers and good pedophiles
with only
the secondary necrophilia
as justification
for the endless, and extremely vile, attacks
against the glory seekers?

Wonder whether, hearing the, oh, children,
of the pain seeker painters

the metaphysical city
is hidden inside the presented paintings

and while the warring hammers
fall onto heads
and the ravines buzz
from the ruin of battle
and the hymns
of fighting saints
the voice is heard:

"Marko Kralle, what do you want?
Here is no play and laughter.
Here are the Balkans"

Andanieus

Gypsy girls dance
however, they don't forget, amid the lust and
circles of the dance
to adorn their long
pitch black hair
with colourful flowers

there are, certainly, three gypsy girls:
one of them is called Theodora
the other Soultana
and the third one
is
the general Theodor Kolokotronis

Erotic Plot

the rain has almost stopped —
will an earthquake come?
vampires keep chiming the bells
while hearts drip blood
in the dark ravines
in strange valleys
of denial where the vanished star,
the companion
of Southern hideouts
Argos

I would like to see it again
as it was
before night falls
and take us to her depth
before the trumpeting of the tempest
declares
the diver was
the lover of the virgins

in the deep glance of reverent male goats
the black clouds of the night gathered again:
green foliage where darkness gleams
they might fight all night long
against the whipping
the hatred
the stubbornness of the rain

(The secret rose blooms
next to the lamp we lit
so that we won't get lost)

come close to the window
and pull aside the dark, heavy curtains
look
the vampires reached
the shore
close to the little wooden house
an ancient god-fisherman
lived

and after they reached the boatbuilders
they decided to build new ships
and cast them in the sea
to leave

they named the first three-masted ship *Earthquake*

Eleanor II

the night raged through the window —
are these, as they call them, the Diocletian Palaces?
I follow your glances over the sea
the secret joys of our body are lying
      on the rocks of the shore
the sun wrapped his highest cypresses
      inside your eyes
let us march into the music of the tropics
the fleshless words of lust and belief rush
Amalekites rush
the galloping horses
the carriage left the road and went through
      the forest
speed and inertia
beautiful daughter of Alesia
haughty, arrogant and profane lovers
      lovers yet
hydraulic saws established here among the red
and green soil of the cypresses
there is the temple of Sophia
further on the bridge, the castle, the cave
      we live in
our bodies will dissolve and vanish
what will remain from us is the I love you I whispered
      during our secret hours

The Hand

For Andreas Embirikos

beautiful net
that the girl weaved
the girl-master
as she
stood by the window in Nafplion
beautiful net
hospitable
like benevolent god
strong
like the white piano keys
of joy
beautiful net
she painted
with the colour of her eyes
and scented
with the aroma of her long hair
the girl that stood
by the window of Nafplion

beautiful net
beautiful girl
a beautiful window that shone
in the Nafplion night
a beautiful window that cried out
a beautiful girl who lighted
beautiful among the colours
of Nafplion

a beautiful net
around
my neck
was
girl
with your beautiful hair
as you comped it
by the window
in the light

beautiful night
in your glance
was the girl
we loved
crazy in love
naked, naked
crazy in love
in the net
of Nafplion

Ten and Four Subjects for a Painting

For Raymond Russell

1. Three men. Two of them sit. The third one, with his beautiful, absentminded glance, his back turned toward the window of the room extends his right arm as if he says something as if he wants to say something.

2. Three men. Two of them stand. The third one sits in the middle of the luxurious room made of ancient marble, of Doric style, with his elbows resting on his knees and his hands on his face. The standing men go near each other and interact with gesticulations and signals, or in a low-tone voice.

3. Three men. Two of them gesticulate as if in a rage or under certain mania. The third man goes to the window and leaning outside, serenely, he tries to discern, in the side street, something hidden from his view.

4. Three men are sitting.

5 Three men are sitting. One of them has a beard and a very nice glance.

6. Three men. Two of them, standing, greet each other at the bus stop "Two friends". The third man wears an army uniform.

7. Three women of exquisite and rare beauty, with a special appearance, dressed in heavy colourful gowns. Two of them sit on gold-adorned tools, with beautiful elbows resting on marble columns of archaic style. The third woman is standing and dressed in a velvet gown of strong red colour, with a big bow, made of expensive satin, on her back. Her name is Maria.

8. Three men on horses inside the room. Dark attire for walking, spurs, whips, helmets.

9. Three silent men inspect a globe. A table is close to them and on it, a hammer, a sickle, an open book, a compass, and other instruments. The sign reads: "Tourists."

10. A garden in the middle of the palace a fountain, cypresses on both sides and a clock. Saint Nikolas, dressed in a chasuble during the mass, holds the Gospel on his left hand and on his right a chart that reads: "Floating over the church of people…" Behind him, are many soldiers and among them Saint George, young and beardless, and the saints Dimitrios, young with curly hair, and Barbaros, carrying chains. On the left of the image, a ship in danger, on the right a ship on its route.

11. Three men, two of them are sitting and gazing straight at the people. The third man, standing, vanishes in the shadow of the far room.

12. Three men. Two of them stand, and the third sits, they display the expression of very busy people.

13 Three men. Two of them sit and face the third man who stands and orates.

14. Three men. Two of them sit, and the third man stands.

The Seventh Love Song

illuminations of love
like wind eavesdropping on a passing cloud
as if the crystal of your tragic eyes
your long hair down to the shore waves
were tied by stars on the harmonious rocks
visions on the prayers of seaweed
onto the light blue slate pencil of the sky
down to the caress of your lively lips
birds fly on songs of hyacinths
the vestiges of the mountain peak darken
the promises of life and joy and joy and life
a harkening musical instrument on your fingers
with the scare and echo of sleep
a fondness of dreams beyond the legs with light
        reflections of roses
by the stairs of lust more and more raving
stand glove bridge of beats psalms spasms
of diaphanous bodies, with the brilliance of lilies,
        that so much tyrannized by thirst
symbols of coves where the sun will reach
        to calm the lust
the last memories of the evening travel far away
how else can you narrate the secret songs
        of the wind
you have sung and will sing and will live
in an ignorant longing, in the flame's reverence
your lit palms define the horizon
your voice caresses the freshness spread by
        the dusk

your body vibrates before the warm pleas
      of the night

and in your glance, joy echoes?

The Last Appearance of Juda the Iscariot

The small American city lost among the endless plains
of Ayrton, lost that serenity it has been familiar with
since the days of around 1867 when it was founded.
Often, around midnight, a strange sullen man entered
the best-secured houses and disturbed the sleeping
people, it stirred their peaceful consciousness, embittered
their hearts with a metal flute he played perfectly, he
awakened in all of them, an intense, tyrannizing and
vague nostalgic emotion. Needless to add, no one
remembered that horrible nightmare when dawn came.
Yet, all day, it was as if a heavy burden fell onto
their souls. Someone, a sleepwalker, solved that
horrendous mystery. One night, just by chance, as
his unsure steps brought him to a beautiful hill,
imposing over the city, he noticed that the bronze
statue of Abraham Lincoln, who usually stood there,
was missing and the marble pedestal lit by the spotlights
seemed deserted. The "President", that bronze
Abraham Lincoln was the strange night visitor!
The sleepwalker was paid a good sum of dollars.
When he was asked, he said his name was Juda.
His last name was Iscariot.

Double Checking the Signals

on the corners of the shadow
the eyes got burned
in the most unbelievable ferocity
of the walls of the zodiac Roxane
lust that charges
as if the result was
never mentioned

hope, curse and flesh
put together the awe
of sleep
they hold the lips
tightly shut
they forget of trickery
in lustful mysteries
the dual salvation
commands

to the dusk the winds raise
the spinning wheel hides us
attracts us
wants the stranger's passion from us
the pain of the material world
in the honeycombs
of yesterday

the rose, like a true styptic
the secret serenity of the day
the fast symbolic tissue
band of light,

of silence
they feel nostalgic
for the escapee who
will be released
and steal and hide
among the leaves
the body
that was truly loved

Flight Example

a woman undresses
in the noise
of alligators
and sows her eyes
and sows her breasts
makes mothers cry
horses neigh
she tops the clocks
deadens the skies
pulls the hoists off her dress
she paints metaphysically
the coffin of the handsome boxer
she swears in the loss of lust

and tomorrow?

Nothing: there is no night without its hail

Chromatic Hero Worship

For N. Kalamaris

a voice is a kerchief
of high tide
under my teeth
in the lie
in the ants' nest of dream
rooms, on a line, in the shade
of wisdom
of the white Bible men

now, a line of rooms and
a bloody tongue of the soul
in the body's reality
unfold the pleats of worlds
that tumble
in a rumble of the light blue

skyward fans
smooth surfaces like before the deluge
loneliness
fire of a black shadow
peaks of glances
a lightning bolt of strength
frenetic horses in the middle of a myriad

earth of three eyelids
ideal waning moon
I reign, stand, forget, remember
black man! Black man!

I row
I loot

oaths of anger by the tower
you painted your two friends
object made of metal and lava
the rest of the secret wall
scale of words, names
the bridge of
the great night
beautiful wife of opium
STRANGELY BEAUTIFUL
sin of love

pure, fiery sperm
patient, unsteady
steady
philosophical
excruciating
how musical, futile
void of thirst

automatic pyramid
rough seas
of lust

Fairytale of the Beautiful of the Big Birds

He put on the gypsy, tin armour and lay down on the new bright, green grass in the light warmth of the spring noon. However, some whispers from outside kept him from getting into the deep lust of the sweetly light blue sky and enjoying the two small clouds that sailed far away at the end of the horizon. There were two very high poplars there too. Indeed, on the north wall, was a heavy partition that hid the door (it wasn't a secret after all). Soon, the door opened, the partition was pulled aside, and a man, wearing a toga appeared in the opening. The poet got up, went close to the porthole and glanced outside while his right hand caressed the back of the lion. "We are close" were the exact words he said, "We are close to Beirut" Suddenly he turned on the faucet and water started flowing, rising in the space dangerously. Then, he runs, grabs her breasts and kisses her lips passionately. He felt a fire spreading in his viscera, a fiery ring wrapping his kidneys while the merciless rise of his penis commenced. *This phallus* strong like marble, was erected at the shore and during the hours of the day, a chorus of girls, embracing each other, crowned with flowers came and sang. Some held hands and with slow steps, created a circle around the idol constantly singing a slow, serious and kind song. One girl walked away from the dance, kneeled and wound a gramophone. The poet was there too. "More pale than the Moon," he said to her.

Memento of Constantinople

on the marble quay of the palace,
they have placed, in an almost straight line,
piles of wood
barges brought from distant
shore forests

and other piles from thin
lissome trunks like a Kore's body
and other piles
of gigantic, huge
trees

it constantly rains and the persistent rain
drenches the graceless woods
and the marble of the quay gleam
as the water washes them repeatedly

and the sky is heavy and black,
one wonders if anyone knows what time it is,
there is no hope for any of that

(The opposite shore has vanished
as if it never existed)

and the sea is moody and wild
as if the endless raindrops that hit it
have awakened a strong anger inside it
that it can hardly hold back

no one else is in this deserted place
other than I, the same one, and
I stand with my drenched red hair
glued onto my forehead

the travails of love have brought me here
to the tender seashore
and my mind always flies to a beautiful
proud magnolia
that thrives and blooms
in this place

Stateless Man Forcefully Exiled

Thus, as he stood, with his nice blonde hair flowing onto his shoulders, handsome, tall, with a helmet, necrophiliac and Aristotelian, with Hermes's cap on his right hand, he looked exactly like the statue of an ancient god. Each time he was at the square, he always had next to him a beautiful naked girl, with a golden, soft body like amber, her long, black hair touching the ground, with the sun and moon painted onto her breasts, with a small depiction of a nightingale on her mound, and two or three red roses embroidered with artistic style on each of her knees. When it happened and he was on a narrow pathway, next to him, he had a naked blonde girl, sitting, and having a bull's head while she played a harmonica. At the harbour quay the girl: red-haired, proud, with fine skin and white like snow, with her name F l u t i s t written in a few places of her body with multicoloured oil paints. Next to a lake: the girl with a harp. Close to the forest: the girl with a scarf. Night in the tavern: beautiful girl, proud and almost half-dead, dressed in luxurious green satin, with a fan, shaped like a ravine or a 7 dancing wild and symbolic dances. During the day he or the girl spent time earning a living. During the night they fought the battle of lust. He would take out a long knife that he put deep in her chest and push it straight down. He'd put his hand deep inside, the girl was always lying on the bed, and he would pull out ribbons, green, red, yellow, light blue, multicoloured, all mixed up which he would raise high up, in a beautiful shape of an offering. From balls of strings, doves flew out, first shyly, uncertain, then flying up to the sky. Now the boat: He would go to the boat, board, take the oars and, standing he would row fast. The girl, always naked, ah, yes: always naked, stood behind him and she had passed her beautiful arms around his neck.

Student of Grief

he started at dawn
to go
and steal
the stars
this statue
started
in the night
and killed
all the
dreams

and as he walked
shoeless
he got caught
in the blackberry bushes
and thorns
bloodied his feet

and his kind, blessed hands
like spring birds caressed
geraniums he named
one Night of love
and her virginal dream interpreter
the heavy buckles

of her breasts
the moans
the red
and the secret
tufts

One Hebrew Girl who Combed her Hair with a Silver Comb

I shall break
your nostalgia
I shall kill
your secret
joy
with
my white birds
that live
and flutter
in your eyes

Eleusis

1948

Past Midnight Cafes and Comets

Travellers came and left
declared enemies of the same forgetfulness
        the same passion
lumberjacks of the same lust
with hearts spread to where the eyes can
        reach
the same black ripped clouds
mix up their masts
rust their anchors
secretly using the conch to whistle the same grief
        into their ears

as if a yellow, golden
bright colour
paints this black and miserable place
mercilessly pierced
by the sleepy lights of electric lamps
the sleepy lights of an ideal, pitiful
        prostitution
and the sleepy *che vuoi* of the wretched camel?

Do you think so?

Think: it is impossible
it is useless to shout and say that
this flame
that eats your viscera
and which you,
yes, you, keep
so well

so tightly
so imprisoned
inside you

the travellers, you'd think, left and came
they solved the riddle
they untied the ropes
that held them tied to the quay
eh, wasn't it?
a dance kindly sad
all these rages of the nostalgic
the wave calms
as it bites in a rage
the net of the dishevelled pines?
the pines that disguised themselves
just for tonight
only
that they won't become comets?

A seabird stretches
its wings
and says:
"you're
the new prophet
in the den of your lions"

The Hawk

A woman's laughter is heard at a distance. A lady laughs somewhere and the wind echoes her laughter here. Up to here, on this deserted shore, under the leaden sky, near the frothy waves, on a position "Three philosophers by the seashore" we live in catatonic loneliness. Wings grow slowly on our shoeless feet. Perhaps we are that winged Hermes in his youth. Ah, that horrible loneliness! Since, there is no doubt that we are alone, all alone, always alone, eternally, painfully alone. All of us. All of us. We, you, all of us. However, I'm the only one who doesn't accept this wretched sentence and I protest, and I hit myself and I shout about it. Only I. And a detail: the lady didn't laugh, she cried. The wind fooled us. The wind changed the sound. Birds fly in the leaden sky. A craft fights on top of the frothy waves. It is far away but it comes closer slowly.

Golden Plataeus

In Gabon
by the banks of the river Ogooue
they made a mask
and who wears it
pretends to be
the moon and the sun
during the dance

for eyes, they put a she-dove
for eyelids, they put the dove complains
for the mouth, they put Bolivar's name
a hole with burning coal
and tears
and holy bones of martyrs
are its beard
and the river Ogooue is its comb and its love

now our boat floats softly on the river
the trees wave to us from the banks
and I hold the mask
on my chest
I recite the prayers of Bithynia
I put my hand softly in the warm water

by the mouth of the river
sharks stare at us with slanting eyes
and swim away
flattery doesn't suit the sharks
flying fish

fly around us
at our command

palm trees
in their regular shape
sometimes like fans
other times like Paraskevas' parasol
during the dance

my bird
is my bird
and I always
love you,
Euthalia Athanasia Thamar Calliope

Odysseus Laertiades

Taking part in performances of a Chinese theatrical
troupe he doesn't refrain from painting his nose with
a brilliant white colour, "a sign of his conniving",
since he doesn't hide his bitterness and shame that
he once was an adulterer. He doesn't make excuses
to his own eyes, or the vertigo he felt from his goal
to reach his Ithaca as early as possible.

Painters and their Landscapes

I, The student of Konstantine Parthenis

Nikos Engonopoulos
if you wish to copy El Greco
focus your mind
on the Cretan mountains

II "Le Fils de L' Ingenieur"

Georgio de Chirico
if you wish to copy
Giorgio de Chirico
don't forget
the shores of Thessaly

A Great Deal of Clearness

In their time, thunderbolts stormed and vanished in
the tempest's heart. And now under the storm, the
animals, patiently in their kingdom, with eyes full of
fields and paths, wait for the hope and flame of Eros.
Rose of the winds, gallows, mistral of rivers and pain,
do what women and birds do. Bring the rich blood
to saunter by the echo of the bell. Bring your hands
like rich cover in the mirror of the seed, strike the
anemones of your long hair and untie the magic of
your eyelids and eyes. Don't you see that the day is
passing fast?

New Laura

the great treasures
about which many talked
of the poor
sick
girl
are only
her lips
her lustful
lips

how I miss them
and glorify them
when I'm away
wandering
on these joyless
unbelievable trips
that so often
I take

however, so much
I enjoy
and glorify them
when I'm
close to her

it is l i f e

it comes out and saunters
in side streets
neighbourhoods

and crying
she calls me
and seeks me

come
don't be like that
we are Hellenes
you are
what a miracle
a girl
a Hellene girl

when I sleep
the flowers of your armpit
come
and caress
my whole body
and when I paint
then
your beautiful eyes
come
to the edge of my brush
and saunter
all over the canvas

so, you know:
I've turned you
into an immortal

Glossary of Flowers

Poetry or glory?
Poetry
Money or life?
Life
Christ or Barrabas?
Christ
Galateia or a shack?
Galateia
Art or death?
Art
War or peace
Peace

Hero or Leandros?
Hero
Flesh or bones?
Flesh
Woman or man?
Woman
Plan or colour?
Colour
Love or indifference.
Love
Hatred or peace?
Hatred
War or peace?
War

Now or forever?
Forever

This or that?
This
You or the other?
You
Alpha or omega?
Alpha
Starting or arrival?
Starting
Joy or sorrow?
Joy
Sadness or boredom?
Sadness.
Man or lust?
Lust
War or peace?
Peace

To be loved or to love?
To love

Glorifying Hymn For the Women we Love

the women we love are like pomegranates
they come and find us
during the night
when it rains
they erase our loneliness with their breasts
they dive deep in our hair
and decorate it
like tears
like gleaming shores
like pomegranates

the women we love are swans
their parks
live only in our hearts
their feathers are
the feathers of angels
their statues are our bodies
the beautiful tree lines are the same
as they are on the tips of their toes
erect
they come near us
as if swans kiss us
on our eyes

the women we love are lakes
among their reads
their fiery lips whistle
our beautiful birds swim in their waters
and then
when they fly away

they reflect
proud as they are
in the lakes
and their shores are white lyres
their music covers our internal
sadness
and fill our essence
with joy
serenity
the women we love
are lakes

the women we love are like flags
and flutter in the winds of lust
their long hair
shine
during the night

in their warm palms, they hold
our lives
their soft bellies are
the sky dome
our doors
our windows
the armadas
our stars always live next to them
their colours are
words of love
their lips are
the sun and the moon
and their sail is the only shroud
that suits us

the women we love are forests
each of their trees a passionate message
in these forests, our steps
trick us
into getting lost
and that's when we find
our true self
and we live
and if we hear the storms coming
from afar
or the wind brings us
noise of celebrations
or the flutes of danger
certainly, nothing can scare us
since thick foliage
surely protects us
since the women we love are forests

the women we love are harbours
(The only destination
of our beautiful ships)
their eyes are
the breakwaters
their shoulders are beacons
of joy
their thighs
line of amphoras at the quay
their legs
are our loving
lighthouses
the nostalgic call them Katerinas
they are their waves

the exquisite caresses
their sirens don't fool us
they only
point to us
the friendly
way
to the harbours: to the women we love

the women we love have a holy substance
and when we hug them tightly
we become the same as the gods
we stand erect like strong towers
nothing can tumble us anymore
they embrace us
with their white arms
and all the people come
nations too
and bow before us
and they cry out
our immortal name
in the eons
since the women we love
transfer
that
holy substance
to us

Reality

The ship entered the αρεα of the thick fog. A bell
echoes desperately at prow: the route is full of
innumerable dangers now. On the bridge, however,
the sleepless and bewildered captain watches and
drives the ship safely. The captain ... his eyes, his
glance. Yes, indeed, his glance is everything, like
now that his glance, straight, strong, mercilessly
pierces through the thick layers of grey pleats of fog
and inside the dark paths of the human psyche, into
the dark sanctuary of Fate, it calms the wildest and
roughest seas, it enters and stands like a guard into
the hovel of the poor fisherman, it saunters tenderly
around the anchors, the sleeping baby, the spread nets
and finally, it comes, settles and serenely rests, next
to the quiet light of the lamp. Certainly, the captain's
profession isn't captain. He has different choices,
different longings, and specialties. Different things
attract him and in different things he's involved. Yet,
when the ship is in danger, they all run to him, who
although they don't see him as a man, they allot to him
and he accepts the responsibility of many souls. He,
who has no joy but knows of it, who isn't free, yet
yearns for freedom and struggles while he hopes.
Let it be known: if the Fates never visited his baby
cradle, Fates, Witches and pure Fairies would come
next to his deathbed. The figurehead of the ship
knows all this and loves him. She's, his lover. This
wild and hot girl with her undone black hair, fiery
red lips and the light-blue belt goes and finds him
secretly every night and they make love 'together'

and chit-chat erotically for hours. One moonlit night:
"Don't forget me", she says to him, "because I'll die"
One day when he was in a thick forest, rain caught up
with him. He sheltered himself in the tree hollow and
waited. The rain intensified. Among all the rain he
noticed a few tree trunks burned by the fires of
wayfarers and many pinecones scattered around the soil.
Another time, a summer noon, he stood by a water well.
Further away was a tower. A girl came, like Rebeckah
to get some water. She puts the pitcher down, goes close
to him, uncovers her voluptuous breasts and says, "Don't
touch them, they are roses and drop their petals; only
caress them" Then again, "No, do as you wish with them,
they are yours, my sweet man, I gift them to you." This
woman, who he fell in love with passionately, one night as
the winds were blowing, he waited for her and he saw
her going down to the harbour. She ran and cried along
the deserted quay. She had tied her raincoat around her
waist with a leather strap and the strong wind sometimes
glued it on her body and other times it whipped her apron
wildly and took away along with her voice, her long
hair too.

Song for the Moon

The old moons, he answered, shattered and became
ightning bolts. Don't you see that when it thunders
they shine like swords?

by Nasrudin

the most beautiful songs
are the moon songs
there are of course
many other
and beautiful
what am I saying,
fantastic songs,
but the most beautiful
we must accept it
are the songs
of the moon

when
tes seins ruissellent d' argent
moons
as you didn't fear the touches,
caresses and questions
of the Nereids
the crowing
night
rooster
doesn't understand
anything
nor the forecast of the weather
they allow to it

or the seals
that dance like ghosts
in the darkness of Delos
that from afar
they look like
cold fires
and smiling
moons

girls with their irises
line their paradisiacal beauty
moons
and line the poets on walls
the other hangs himself talking
of endless verses
and squeezes his heart
like a sponge
blood drips with silver
reflections
moons

the grandmother knits the glove
the crazy man measures the storm
smoke of the universe
like a crown
once they enriched life
and now tugs of death
how they silence
the pale flowers of Epitaphios
you, oh, moons

I'll come to the secret memorial
service of your anger
silent and coverless
with hands to count the years
I'll whip the snow
from inside your eyes
that shine of naphtha and stars
small tree lines dancing
to the cries of your sold-out fiancé
to be filled with
the white black
the moon
hangs on your hair

I know, it will never return
the little that remains
of life
of moons close to you
roses of the winds
narcissists of the fog
the fountains
shimmer
music of loss and contempt
raise your hands
let us collect
the saintly waters
of a special wisdom
that grace
those who passionately implore
the moons

this song somehow produces sadness
to the person who reads it
and to the one who hears it
though we never hid it from anyone:
if the most beautiful songs
are naturally the saddest
songs written
for the moons
exception of the rule,
write it down,
are the songs written
close to a cataract
and others sung
on a sinking ship
while the siren with the dishevelled
hair accompanies it
and others sang
         by a Kore with a harp
under the plucked statue
of an old goddess
and flooded
by the moons

close the blinds and listen to the passerby
the steps you hear
is the rising moon
think of the sea and go to sleep
think of lust and wake up
undo her hair
         and flood it
with moons

the moons behind the trees
like piano trills reminding of Hellas
with her flutes, harbours and legends
Genevieve enjoys
her lover Erotokritos
the pitcher of Plato
they took to the well
slipped off his hands
and scattered around in pieces
(Among the beech trees of the ravine
sacrificial lambs, guerillas)
rosewater and sperm
become one
when the moons
flood Hellas

you sleep and your eyelids
and breasts excite
the crafty archers at the embrasures
here we are again
in the plain
at Examili
my hand is the trough for your wash
and I hear from up close
the grief that ravages your breast
your song
my erotic dove
while
over the sponges
the moons
shine

over the roofs, chimneys
morning *ladies*
with such laziness and charm
wait for the passing of the autumnal birds
many flocks of birds
as if writing a special letter on the sky
the letter each person expects
on the chimneys,
are two doves
under the chimneys, are
two doves-hands
that throw white flowers,
perhaps camellias or gardenias,
over your enchanting steps
oh magical
moons

ride the horse, oh rider Saint George
you'll find jewels in the chest
you will bring
to save the lilies of virgins
however
when you pass the lakes
say words of love
to the waters
that reflect
moons

manes-gods chime the bells
in the gardens
the moons shine
multilayered threat calyx of sin

filthy palaces artichokes of regret
I knock at your door
come open
and show
your endless beauty
to the moons

moons hang off your eyebrows
and go down
and a fiery broadsword
behind the mountain
the new Zeus.
Squeeze our hearts:
sweat will pour
the holy sweat of the worker
unjustly killed
and the moon is
the blade of the knife

slavery, correctly, means bitterness
come, all of you,
cross yourselves
(A cross never
goes to waste)
look,
but look quickly:
the moon goes down

Poetry 1948

this season
of the civil war
is not time
for poetry
if something
is written
it is as if
it was written
on the other side
of death
announcements

for this reason
my poems
are so sad
(Besides, when weren't they?)
and they are
especially
just a few

Atlantic

1954

Pleasantly we cross the ocean…
                                    Psalm
        Who are we? Where are we going?
                                    Paul Gaugin

the ship echoes
the train whistles
they give the signal
from the little towers
careful
the voyage starts
come
we depart
for a foreign land

at the café of the Albanian cobblestone square
lost among the crowd
of the serene
undisturbed usual square
into which morality
silence and decorum
reign,
we won't stay longer
the voyage calls us
come: we depart
for a foreign land

the reveries in the side streets
of Peiraeus stopped
the night doesn't find us in a familiar
neighbourhood
when the lights turn on

when the kids yell
tender corners don't find us
by the quay
the dead facades of beautiful buildings
don't seek the shape of our polite bodies
yesterday's display windows are
an insult to us
we leave the same as always
we depart for a foreign land

rhythm isn't our goal anymore
the goal has escaped out of our door
in the churches, the chandeliers are turned off
and the candelabras that light the icons
the women's quarters vanish in darkness
into which women frequented
and before the altar the big candle
starts the vigil
however, we are called by the foreign lands
and as soon as dawn comes
we depart for the foreign land

the hat maker matches feathers and live birds
fresh flowers on the hats
the postman is tired of his come-and-go
the milkman prepares
the evening yogurts
and the beautiful virgin still knits by the window
in a while, she will let her needle down
and place in her curly hair the crown of grief
as she is about to drink in one gulp
the poison she has prepared since morning

the faucet drips, the pitcher fills
                  the miller turns the mill
                  the moon reigns, Venus will rise
we depart for a foreign land

we placed the most awaked man
at the helm
on the smokestack
we put a bayadere
and our chairs are rococo:
hey, we'll pass the Atlantic!
Storms and rain will hit us
and, like them or not,
what rough seas and what bad luck!
Waves will charge to sink us
thunderbolts will whip the sky
saltwater will drench us
as if we were under a faucet!
Yet, let it be known we'll make it
no one
will drown
as the foreign land
expects us

calm seas and sunshine blue sky, not a single cloud
the waters are calm dark green
like a painting of Altamira
we shall enjoy the serenity
while we lean over the deck
and we shall see the whalers follow
their precious hunt
        and no concern, no shiver

despite the heavy atmosphere
and, as everything changes, here is the fog
the ship enters the fog area
impossible to see ahead of us
curtains of fog in layers
and the first raindrops
start falling
and a sudden, wild wind starts
to ruin the sails
the boats the masts
it destroys everything on the ship
it groans around us like a beast
and the wooden ship rocks
how far the images of our homeland —
under us, the abyss opens
and darkness thickens in the horizon
as if it was possible
it thickens
darkness falls
dawn comes
curtains of rain replace the partitions of fog
the bright sun is hidden
and only the cursed wind
ravages the palm trees in the faraway islands
our ship delays
it delays a lot
when are we to arrive
to the foreign land?

The Atlantic, I repeat surrounds us
it's a huge ocean
we are timid it is fearsome

it throws us around like shells
and in our ears, it whispers
frightening messages (it threatens us)
by God, let us not lose our courage!
Boys have hope for our fate!
Soon, soon
will it appear
the foreign land
to where we are headed.

Discussion:

Man, you who suffer
all alone, what do you seek
in the endless ocean?
Why aren't you afraid of drowning?
Or the least, you may be late
reaching
the foreign land.

Answer:

You tell me that whether
I get lost or drown
or that I may be late to reach
but what else could I do?
Thus
        they
                threw me
                        into
                                the ocean

the voyage unfolds based on a prearranged
route
is there any belief?
What can we do with the wonder
about such constant exchange
of rough and calm seas
of the tempest and serenity?
What's its use?
We shall go somewhere
we shall go somewhere
but for a while
I'm very sorry
think of it
what can we do
if the foreign land
doesn't exist?

We are now in the ocean

On a Flowery Hellenic Logos

1957

Memory

I untie her hair, dive my hands into her lovely locks
and my laughter echoes over mountains, valleys,
ravines and peaks full of eternal snow. Her pleading
eyes break my heart: I must uproot trees again, must
let the water flow freely in the ditch. The beautiful
dark-skinned girls must come and spray their breasts
with the water of the rosy fountain. Must, must, must …
I crush the rose of joy between my kind hands. I open
the birdcage so the birds fly away, freely, at night.
An angel pops up from the sink. I welcome him,
I offer him stamps, figs, lion skins, and kisses. I stand
by the front step of the villa. I always search the horizon
and leaning down, I try to clean the glass of the lens
with my fingers, so the moon may come and rest on it.
Suddenly the voice:
"Nikos Engonopoulos, you shouldn't have done this"
We all sit and cry around the table with the red cover
until one fruit bowl with wrinkled fruits reminds us
the futility of human expectations, and of hope too.

Mrs. Urania

She, who certainly exists in the snow-covered dwelling
in Byzantium, can't play in the country shooting ranges
with the many superstitions of popular regiments of
Western monks. Its prospect is unpleasant, its pragmatism
wrong, the point of 6500 meters in height has many fans,
however, so that no one could sense the size of her loss, the
comments of her children are not enough, the assurances
of her innumerable lovers, the conclusion of Kolkhozes
of her infidelities. The cuffs of Hagia Sophia, the nation's
hope, *the drink of plains*, here is the evidence in her defence,
always forgotten, that we want to underline in a desperate
effort for expiation and awe. Her name is Euterpe. Don't
tell me that she wasn't worthy of the tears you shed on her
apron, the reverent incense of passion we burned to the
image of her breasts, the lit candle we occasionally offered
to the memory of the feathers she used to adorn her hats
with. Thus, the fantasizing of the *lawless* aren't needed
here, at this time. The night temperature doesn't dare
anything against the deadly traps or fishing. Homeland of
democracy is the Arc and the eulogy.

Orpheus the Xenophobe

the tears stain life

have you cried so much
and now your eyes are dry
oh women
of Hellas?

there where your eyelids fell
cypresses flourish
and always on their tops
a bird

Lover

He talked in a different language, the dialect of a forgotten, now, city, of which, only he felt nostalgic.

Mercurio Bua[*]

He kneels and opens the chest and while he holds the cover
with one hand the other searches for something in it.
"What do you have?" I ask him.
He turns:
"Lettere d'amore," he says.
And then:
"You don't care?"
"Of course, you know, since it refers to love," I answer.
Then with careful movements, he took the items, one by
one and showed them to me. Firstly, he pulled up and
showed me various velvet fabrics, a pile of clothes, some
embroidered, some discoloured. Then, a rotten mattress,
and finally he lets the cover, takes out a well-kept corpse of
a man and puts it on the floor. What was most important
about the corpse was its smooth and shiny skin and unkept
hair as well as the warlike, long moustache.

---

[*]   *Count of Aquino and Roccasecca*

Arcesilaus

he left
and I see him
distancing
along
the deserted avenue
and often he turned
and waved
with the imperceptible
movement of his eyebrows
until
slowly
his stature
vanished
at the end of the horizon

he wrote

in his letter
he said, among others
that he loved
the rain

"I'm a Hellene,
were his words,
my motherland and mother
is the rain

when rain catches up with me,
he continued,
when it finds me

naked
walking around
it dresses me,
the rain,
with unbelievably shining
outfits
as I walk,
      and places around me
mythical riches
sets
and decorations"

he now saunters to the "end"
among the crowds, music and popular joy
and mixes
becomes one with
the crowd

and feels
sometimes
like a king among his subjects
and other times
perhaps the same moment
like
an exiled ruler
among
strangers
and unfamiliar
people

About Height

The Italian pyrotechnic has established his humble and
poor workshop on the top of an Attica hill. He keeps busy
there, day and night, with his many experiments and the
creation of his products: fireworks, copper engravings
and other things, since, on the day before each Christian
celebration, he provides the crowd with these creations
and again during the nights of the national anniversaries
he decorates our skies with various fantastic flowers,
with awe-inspiring decorations and the fastest rockets
which end up in multi-coloured rain of sparkles. Rarely
did he leave his work, yet, during the nights, he carries his
ravaged and mixed-up silhouette from tavern to tavern,
preferably going along the dark side streets of the agora.
His profession is dangerous: gunpowder, which means
dynamite is the first material he uses. The tiny carelessness
is enough to create a catastrophe: in the thundering burst,
the workshop and the worker is blown into the clean
morning, and we see them swirling in the air for hours,
both the Italian and the planks of his shack along with
thick clouds of dust while a strong smell of gunpowder
spreads around.

Yet, the fateful event never happens since there is, a
secret: this secret is truly the wife who watches over. Truly,
his wife is one of us: reverent Orthodox Christian, day
in and day out she's in churches, bows to the ground and
always prays for him. This keeps him alive.

In fact, in the crevasse that surrounds the Attica
sky, there, the unfortunate woman has spread numerous
icon stands, most of them made of marble, others a little
humble, but all of them with an icon of the Virgin Mary

or some other saint and a little door for the donations. She goes on regular visits to collect the money which she uses primarily for donations to various charities but she keeps certain part of it since she plans to one day build a church in the name of Saint Catherine.

(Further on, down in the crevasse, someone has placed some beehives in a field and further on in the orchard are the ruins of the tumbled stately estate.)

This story of the Italian is our story, Helen. Am I not a pyrotechnician? My poems are Easter copper engravings, and my paintings are of unbelievable beauty and superb creations of the Attica sky. However, if they haven't ripped me apart yet to throw my flesh to the dogs, this I owe to you, to your great care and love. I know it, don't hide it from me, I know when I say: you pray for me.

Collect the money from the icon stands and spend it with your saintly, white hands, spread goodness all over. However, save some, so that we can save a small amount to build a church dedicated to the Queen who carries your name. I'll get married to you in there, in that church, because you are beautiful and have the kindest, and most proud soul and I love you passionately.

For Rent

inside this room
he let his last breath
the beautiful Athenian girl
laid on silk sheets
het blond undone hair on the pale head
while through the open window
the bells of Saint Saviour
were heard
chiming
the evening matins
the next morning
was the celebration
of the prophet Samuel

inside this room
the two fearful beasts made love
and enjoyed
with moans and wild grunts
and wild shouts
as if Bulgarian lumberjacks
fought against gigantic fir trees
or rather
(b e t t e r)
mountains were
tumbling

inside this room
the old lady
spent her years
in boredom

she could stir
her shaking hands imperceptibly
trying in her foggy mind
to recall images of her past greatness
to the day
that with slow steps
she moved,
they moved her,
to the old folk's home

three children were born
inside this room,
descendants of an honourable family
that vanished
no none of them ever lived,
one of them emigrated to America
the other had a horrible death, a drunkard,
and the third one
is still somewhere
as a lighthouse keeper

here, yes, inside this room
an immoral hand murdered
that brave man
to punish anarchy personally,
he said,
and the poplar leaned and died
and that foggy stain
on the floor
there by the corner
is the blood that was shed,
like a river, from the wound

and nothing could
ever wash it off the planks

yet enough is enough: what am I doing?
it would be tiring
perhaps impossible
surely endless
and futile even boring
to narrate with such detail
the endless
history
of this room

Sometimes they brought beds inside
other times they took them out
sometimes there were blinds
sometimes a closet
or a chest
other times the windows had only cloth hanging
other times the windowpanes were empty
only with the shutters
they had a few icons in that corner
other times they had many pictures

here it is: many men came in and went out
many others were born in here
others were placed in their coffin
laments, cries
joyous voices
baptisms
silent desperation
and weddings

(I almost forgot it: a piano echoed in here too
playing softly the Romance du Mal'Aime)

I, too, lived in this room
for many years, poorly as always
and here I passionately got busy
with painting and poetry
sculpture
but philosophy too and Eros
I remained sitting for hours
smoking
by that window
looking
sometimes in the sky
and other times on the road

and now I must, alas, leave too
perhaps better things are meant for me

they are renting the room again

Goodness of People

lift the lamp
look into the mirror
poor woman
you notice
your empty
eye sockets

(And from afar
the echo
yells:
Eurydice)

About the Death of the Spanish Poet Federico Garcia Lorca on the 19th of August 1936 in the Ditch on Camino De La Fuente

…una accion vil y disgraciado

art and poetry don't help us live
　　　art and poetry help us
　　　die

absolute disdain
fits
all noises
research
comments over comments
that often state
the unemployed vain writers
under mysterious and lewd conditions
of the execution of the fateful Lorca
by the fascists

but finally: everyone knows
that
for a long time
especially during these bad years
they make it a habit
of murdering
poets

Clelia *Or Better*

The Lagoon Love Affair

I

you have human eyes
and the life
of children
your fine waist
cries on all
my dreams
you give me the joy of eagles

you don't regret it, do you?
You won't regret
that we left and went
to the lagoon's green-blue peace
look, so as you have the time,
at the distancing
square
all the crowds
saunter
with their shitty coats
the impious people,
walk in a circle
you won't regret it
I repeat
we won't miss, you won't miss
anything
since we went
far away

I love you and pull your long, red hair
to your white, thin legs
the nipples of your breasts inspire me
and standing
with steady hand
I drive the boat
toward the islands
where they throw piles
of bones and craniums of the dead

on the blond sand
of the shore,
a beautiful bed waits for us
the river reeks and
verdure surrounds it

(Indeed, you and I
existed there like running creeks
only that I
was an extra
idolizer
and punisher
of her)

II

don't cry, sweet one, don't cry
for the days that passed
were, know it, the gift of gods

the earth is silenced
and before the sun we love goes down

and it doesn't plan to rise again
I'll take you
by your file hand
to walk ahead

you see that monument
over there
we'll open the door
and walk inside
I'll embrace you in there
and thus in each other's arms
we shall vanish
into the colourful gleam
of the Second Coming

Marcinelle

the pigeons are asleep now

and the cyclone rages
amid the wild rustle of the trees
follows the suspicious silence
thunder and cannons echo in the distance
and here it rains
and rips everything
the foliage screams
trees stand ready to leave
and among the wild blackberry bush
opened just like a bare-breasted
old woman
the lighting
reveals
two rotten tree trunks
lying in the mud
bodies of two lovers
with bare branches like arms
that stir
curses
or moans
learn to live

by the peaceful edge
is the bread and the steaming pot
here is the knife
take the knife to cut the bread

take the knife
take the knife, I tell you, worker
tonight
be extra careful, tonight
t h i s n i g h t i s n o t l i k e o t h e r n i g h t s

Marcinelle, 1956

In the Valley with the Rose Gardens

1978

Experience

Letter to a pseudo-philosopher and a by-chance prayer

We must catch the wolf inside his hole, in his den. We must drag him out in the free air. To put a line of bright, decorative stars on his forehead and replace his hatred for the people with fiery love in his heart. But, how, Lord, you believed that we could call it a success, a big success at that, that you filled your viscera with vanity, greed for show and imposition, with great avarice in this narrow space of your experiment or even far from it? But how, Lord, can you forget the sorry state of your Creation? No, man deserves to live with his head up, his bare chest, his wide-open heart to every request that may arise around him. Just like the wolf we mentioned, in his den.

A Rather Pessimistic Sonnet

would the expert eye of the thud
discern the rhododendron's harmony?
No, no, an endless morality won't
help us change the world into a better one

to hope, to always hope, that among the people
who the horrible convenience ravages,
you'll meet soft souls with manners
full of goodness, longing for kindness, and serenity

perhaps not too many, if you're unlucky: none!
then you try to become better
in a way that some balance may arise

let all around you get busy to do something
you think — now, with what sweet serenity
you anticipate the time when you'll lie down
onto the consoling deathbed

Poem-Imitation of Many Psalms for Male Choir In Ecclesiastical Music of Johann Sebastian Bach

curse him, oh Lord, who stole
the bread of the poet
curse him, Lord, who put his impious hand
in the meagre amount of money
of the poor painter
who stole coins
from the stretched
humble
hand of the beggar
curse him!

let the bread become poison
                    and waste
and the stolen coin
fiery nail in the merciless breast
of those who committed crimes
who acted unjustly against the poor widow
who hit the unprotected child
who broke the clay dish of the thirsty man
who denied care for the sick man
who tricked the leper
who hit the crazy man
and fooled the blind
who made the life of frail difficult
the perjurious
the infidels
who tortured Hebrews and Christians
in the concentration camps in Germany

there is God

the day passes
the hour passes
society laughs
the excuses are retained
yet, the one who committed
the crime and went to sleep
didn't sense
that dawn came and he woke up
and walked about
in the horrible darkness of death
(his mouth is already full of dirt)
and of the one who lied
and acted unjustly
and slapped
they will pay for it and their children
will do so too
up to the fifth generation

there is God

hearts and kidneys are examined
and next to the crippled justice of man
the Fury hides
nested deep in the guilty man
merciless and unforgiving
who doesn't care about officialities and titles
that good life brings but in God's name,
it doesn't care and it punishes
harshly
the brainless and timid who commit

a crime
because

there is God

hey, you perjurious man
you, who lied in court
who harmed your neighbour
with the lightness of conscious
you already hear the psalms
of your funereal procession
the conniving laughter
of the sarcastic pneuma
hey, liar citizen no matter how hard
you try to show us
your face as benevolent
don't waste your time:
the dirt covers your face
of your lonely soul
and the cowardice
and lies

there is God

as the just man's wealth
will become a gift from God
the lawless man, don't worry, will be judged
listen to the words of the poet:
the lawless bread is of no use
there is God, certainly

yet how bad that there are so few men!

For the Death of the Anthologist of True Love

How did you waste your last night again? In which regrets
did you bow, to which temptations did you succumb?
I understand you, I see it in your teary eyes, in your
tears that dried your heart and skin and turned them,
unfortunate man, into chirps of birds, into dried-up
bacalao hanging off the middle mast to replace the
flags of many boring fanaticisms. Bring here the two
black diamonds you hold in your hands, they are love!
And throw away what you hold in the pocket of your
undergarment: it is the ledge of sin, the anguish that eats
up the viscera of the passionate, the Arch of Triumph
through which they carried your cadaver, Benjamin Peret.

Pleading

The night follows the day. And as the day is the space
of trees and flowers, the night is the space of ghosts and
hydrants. You put the ladder against the wall and carefully
pass to the other side. You sense whispers, like the rustle
of dead leaves and the flow of waters, the imperceptible
sound of the mill's wheel. A wheel, a plough, stars and
the miracles and the magic of night begin. With your lips
glued on her white legs, think of it, tell yourself that you'll
never stop begging, you'll never stop calling up all the love
you have hidden inside you, against the forces of evil.

The Image

the dogs bark in the night
the deep shade of the trees
the morning chirp of the skylark
the song of the water flowing from the spring
the reward, the only one,
for the exhaustion
the laments
the wounds
of those who the storm caught
those who the conniving spirits tyrannized
those who felt
painfully of course
all the hues of
both the colours and feelings
the cawing of agony
and the soft whimper of the dove

let us place the flowers where the beast stood
let us drive the true lovers of truth to the benevolent artesian wells

let us swear that we shall never die

The Cradle the Oil Lamp

I always loved
passionately
every expression of life
but I wasn't concerned
with death

now that you let me rest
next to the bright light
of your beautiful eyes
now I love you more than life
and I wouldn't like
to ever die

The Letter

a bird was chirping
like they sing a lullaby to a baby
and the golden ring was blessed by
and those who count my dreams

in the taste of the week's bread
they cut the thread in two
games of love and lust?
How far from us are the rivers?

we safeguard the house well
with lances and swords
and the plane trees of beautiful ships
stir in the morning like kisses

and while it is still Sunday
on your moon-like hair: forests of jasmines
our primeval sin goes down
to the sarcasm of the cheeks' absence

the mouth has these echoes
the manly blood has that smell
sign of tenderness in the foggy glance:
come, let us tell the truth to the children

what our hand touches
under the sky of our other motherland
is the blessed wheat and the caress
opened by the spring of love

it is love that entraps the night
pours stars in the secret bosom
that throws away the pebbles (the dry wood pieces)
so that you'll never find the road too long

we shall pass with partridges on our side
with a song like a bloomed rose
we shall always share a pillow
and from the same palm, we shall always drink water

About the Pious Hebrews

the rabbi of Nuovo Ghetto
is my friend.

he shows a special fondness for
the red-haired little boy
that I was once
as he saw me
so much focused
to his narratives
about the unparalleled achievements of Judaism

sometimes, rarely, of course, he stops,
his trust shaken,
he stops and
looks at me:
who am I after all, but a foreigner?
However, he soon composes himself,
and continues:
there is of course the legend of Alexander the Great

the verger is Ukrainian,
he's a priest too,
his father was, he boasts about it,
an executioner
he too comes from
the Levi family
yet his career in the priesthood
hierarchy got stuck because of a few scars
he has on his face,
results of his wild childhood,

that doesn't allow him
to stand before
the Eternal
the thrice blessed and
Horrible

the rabbi's daughter meets me
every evening
by the shore
and each evening, with lowered eyes
she informs me
of her love

it seems that I wasn't indifferent to
the scimitar-eyed Hebrew girl:
she'll often appear
in my future poems
always attractive
and graceful
and beautiful
and certainly
each time with a different name
sometimes as Laia
other times as Rebekka
and other times as Esther

The Flag

don't disregard love
the crying eyes aren't beautiful
however, don't delay:
you'll come back soon, won't you?
each time I dare something
that cloud of hope comes
with white and soft rosy tricky lace.
Be serious:
it's impossible to set the guillotine daily
slowly your hair will turn white:
white flag.
The other flag is the sign
that you give up and that the castles
tumble forever

Harmonica

I'll always see my mother
as young and beautiful
as she was

tall, blonde
with the sweet
and softly sad
glance

standing in front of the full-size mirror
checking her exquisite trendy
attire

as she plans
to go out soon

from the open windows
the room fills with
serene morning light

next door a childish harmonica
plays a soft
joyous
celebratory song

Flowers

eyes that don't see anymore
glances that don't get attracted
by the world

you are stars

you light the world

Merope

It's the impossible of impossible
to win over time

love adds purity
and this fiery love
we showed
we offered
was seen as a weakness and such

now, the colours:

of the light blue sky
the green of the trees
the foggy of the mountains
elements of the composition
for the beautiful
exquisite
painting of life

Close your Eyes: All Your Old Life Will Parade in front of you

For Memas Messinis

When I was passing, unsuspectedly on a gondola, someone called me.
"Hey Hellene, hey Hellene…"
He was standing behind the iron Gate of the grassy court-yard of Saint George of the Hellenes, next to the canal.
"Hello to you too," I said, "what brings you here?"
"I'm dead," he says.
"Well," I said, "blessed man, you a Hellene why did you die here? Why didn't you go to die there, in our soft, homeland soil?"
"I would love it" he answered. Besides, one night, Natalia from the Laggon, told me so, you remember her, the girl with the golden breasts. She took me aside and said: "take me away from here, I can't live with the bastards, You, see, her mother was from Smyrna. However, the other one, the blonde and beautiful harlot kept me here, the one who worked at the pigsty of Fretseria. She would passionately sing up to the evening, the song "Even if you are far away" that sweetened my lips and broke my heart.

Surrealism of Eternal Life

For Tristan Tzara

The cradle of the poet
is his coffin
and the rattle
they put in his baby hands
is the cypress
that will grow
on his grave

because
despite all the grief they feed him,
the poet
carries the denial of death in him
even more so,
he is the denial of death

thus
the coffin of the poet
will become his cradle again
and the cypress of his grave
will be his rattle
which he will brandish
in his sunlit hands

Life is a Dream

around the trunk
of the beautiful tree
swirls
and dances
the beautiful
gypsy

the tree is fully bloomed
but the body also
of the beautiful gypsy
therefore:
from the flowers, the nipples of her breasts
the shine of her soft belly
the round buttocks
the impeccable thighs
the bushy forest of her mound
the flowing hair
undone and waving freely
sparkling in the night
spreads her heavy perfumes

the tree is a big magnolia
and the beautiful gypsy
is also a magnolia
juicy
rich
lustful

which is more beautiful
the beautiful tree
or the beautiful body?

The beautiful body
because while the tree stays always mute
that the strongest winds can't
shake off the heavy leaves and fleshy flowers
the beautiful body
comes and goes
it gets drunk intensely
branches and truck
vibrate

in the most silent
whisper
of
I love you

Ballad of a Tall Ladder

Episode from the life of painter Theophilus

In every city, Appollinaire said, there are some
immortal people. You may be one, mister, among them,
or even you, sir. I don't know. I can certainly
assure you of one thing: that there are. Perhaps
a few. Surely, there are.

Theophilus once climbed
a tall ladder
witnesses claimed
perhaps to paint a sign
or perhaps to complete
the upper part
of his heroic composition

street kids
who in time
as it was natural
grew into adulthood and old age
(they didn't remember anything anymore)
and they died
as famous
and peaceful citizens
street kids, I repeat,
in order to have some fun
they pulled
the tall ladder

and as Theophilus fell
in horrible fear
from the heights
he expected to become a crippled man
or even worst
to die on the soil

but, what a miracle
he landed
safe and in one piece
(Although one of his feet was injured
and he limped for the rest of his life)

but I repeat
in one piece
from top to bottom
because of the fall
only his humble clothes
turned golden like the Sun
his face
they said pale, like the Moon
but lit like the Moon
these two stars
usually co-exist
in icons of Byzantine Art

and if he went to hide in Mytilene afterward
he was already immortal:
it was meant to live forever

I m m o r t a l

Perhaps along with his clumsy co-citizen
Giorgio de Chirico
and with Benaroya
among many
others
some from Volos
who lived before
and during
and after
the pulling of the ladder
era

Dialogue Excerpt

The Fighter

no, people aren't bad, he says
don't forget the old saying
made to the likeness of the Lord

certainly, there are some foolish among them
who believe in evil acts
they try to affect harm to their likes
they live
and act
to express their existence strongly

I met many such people
and you understand
they bothered me a lot
they harmed me and made my life difficult
as I had surely devoted it
with passion
to those difficult issues
for me anyway
of chromatic combinations
and harmony

On Boeotian Roads

careful: this Oedipus
we are to meet
at the fork of Boeotian roads
no: he's not the mythological Oedipus

despite the forever elephantiasis
the gout, the acromegaly
he suffers from
I tell you he has nothing to do with the old Oedipus

He hasn't killed his father,
go and tell it to Iocasta,
he's not to get married to his mother

leave him alone and he'll move on
and then, soon enough, he'll vanish forever

but that black dog
lying in the middle of the sunlit road
sunlit from the sun that will go down
asleep or dead among the donkey poops
eh, he's something

remember it: the dog is the Sphinx of the myth
that tumbled
when she realized
that her secret
didn't exist anymore

Poem for Georg Trakl

For Kyriakos Kariopoulos

It seems the poplars are done with
the rain that harassed them all morning

it is night now:
as if someone stopped the rain
it still drizzles a little
you vaguely hear the rustle among the leaves

through the skylight of the neighbouring building
rises, thickened, tough
that same monotonous and persistent musical phrase
of someone, perhaps the caretaker's
who in his basement abode
persistently learns to play the ocarina

the thought of the weak may go and stand over
the wide open plains of Western Macedonia
where the poplars (again poplars) on an endless line
betray, in the forlornness, the flow of the long rivers

the mind likes to be next to
the wide and deep Danube
in Vienna
and there, the eyes of the soul filled with passion
will try to bring it back in front of them
the vanished face
of the poet
his slanting glance

Georg Trakl, as if in the famous Salzburg
of the Austrian Tyrol, where he saw the light
for the first time,
he never found joy anywhere, never

he spent his childhood in boredom
as he anticipated the time of knowledge
which arrived, it'd be better if it didn't,
when he lost his mind
yes: he never agreed with them, the proud man
never accepted
the fate and habits people have

as soon as he realized, painfully enough, what means
to be alive
he had no other longing but to escape, to go away

that longing, his grief you could say, never left him
nothing could console him
nothing entertained him, nothing made him
forget for a while

not Vienna
with its wide avenues
the beautiful cafes
the gardens the lakes with ducks
not even the legendary
innumerable beauties
the hidden
and truly unforgettable treasures

in vain the Dyadic Monarchy
that sent him to the war of 1914
trying tenderly to make him forget
like tender parents apply the lobotomy
to their insubordinate children
in vain, I repeat

he was looking for the time, what am I saying,
the hour, the moment
and he sadly said it in his songs
to get rid of this inhumane way of life
the sorrowful problem
the ugly anguish
and to go somewhere
faraway
to go
somewhere else

and he managed, finally, one evening: simply
tant l'on crie Noel qu'l vient

Poem for Gregory Patsikian

don't ever say that they fooled us
no
that's life, simply, Gregory

and they found Leda without her swan
Medea without her poisons
or medications
Scheherazade not knowing a myth

Sphinx without a riddle
men without joy
and all the hatred

as we started, we tried or not
to convince the world
and firstly ourselves
that never mind:
things aren't as they are

and we tried, we fought
we struggled
for this purpose, all our lives
without any reservation
we have spent it
passionately

without letting our minds ever go
to all these efforts of ours
the gestures
the shouts

like all others around us
we did it by the edge
of the black hole
that gaped under our feet since the first day
we saw the light
the black hole, I repeat
of our grave
Gregory

City of Light

to John Pappas, sculptor

On this side of the train tracks, beyond the grain fields, at the feet of the high mountain, the beautiful Hellenic city extends among the fields and the gardens. A Hellenic city since the ancient days. Just before autumn, the hill is hit by storms and rains. It looks white on the first winter days as it is covered by snow. The waters freeze. I mentioned that the city is Hellenic. It is strange too. It is adorned with beautiful buildings representing all the epochs of the nation's history. The buildings are maintained well, only a small repair is needed here and there for their unique and impeccable look. The strange thing about the city is that alive and dead people live together in this city in harmony. Thus, despite the emigration of the people, to the point that the rest of the county is deserted, the city continues to be populated. Once, during my travels, I happily passed by there. How can I describe my joy when I met my father there, whom I hadn't seen in many years but with Skendempei, countess Nollaig, the philosopher Empedocles, the holy Marquis de Sade, Mozart sitting by his piano, Odysseus Androutsos, Rigas Velistinlis, with his bouzouki and many other familiar people.

Cricket

the banner, the flag
of life and day
is enriched
with multicoloured ribbons
beads
and long
red tassels

the multicoloured ribbons
are the joys
our songs
are our dreams
that accompany us on deserted shores
they are barrel organs
playing under the trees
when we saunter in the forest
they call us explanations
of the rain

secrets are lit
by dazzling lightning bolts
the axes split open
the evil intends
and the world echoes
with voices
of children
satyrs
and Ghirlandajo

the beads are chairs of cafes
that forbid
the passionate
discussions
about politics
and playing backgammon

and when the heavy burdens
arrive
then the tassels take charge
the worries scatter
away from us
as if by a miracle
the clouds vanish
the sun shines again
the tears dry up
the sirens stop
and free again
we toss around
in the tugboats
and crafts
of lust

bells chime
in the neighbourhoods of the city
in the side streets of Truba*
the guitars
create havoc
as they narrate

---

*   *Piraeus neighbourhood famous for its brothels*

the achievements
of lizard killers
in myths
and the West comes
and everything
is lost

Timon the Athenian

he imagined himself
like a scrubby wolf
as all the people
around him barked
like dogs with rabies

but finally, he understood
how late, oh, God,
so late
that it always
happens like that:
people attack
wildly and mercilessly
against each isolated man
same as the dogs
with rabies

Brief Biography of the poet Constantine Cavafy and Everyone Else's

there is no ship for you, no way out
                    C. P. Cavafy

anguished and burdened
he saunters the narrow side streets
of the joyless city
that eats his viscera

in which he was born
in which he'll die
bitterness he drank
and tyrannized him
all alone
sometimes he believed
certainly rarely
that he found joy

once he too wished
to go someplace far away
but he went to the shore
and the ship had departed

A Somewhat Aged and Brave General Yet Young Looking and Vigorous

every morning at about the same time the general
who lives in the neighbouring building goes out.
The jeep that will take him has arrived since dawn
and the soldier with crossed arms walks with wide
straddle around the car, until he stops at once and
stands in attention when the general appears. The
general, of some age, is short yet well-attended,
nervous, youngish-looking, and very brave. The
red ribbon around his cap doesn't mean
that he'll be named fallen for the homeland. True
to his duty, he seems merciless regarding rules
and regulations and the black book, unbending
about the enforcement of these army rules. Yet,
he has kept his whole leniency for his exclusive
use. I'm saying ...

Difficulty

I was lucky
in my life
to meet many
good and always
correct people

perhaps they were more austere than normal
perhaps, how can I say it,
even a little tough
but isn't this the right
of those who know
and know how to judge
everything?

The difficulty arises when no one
of the just people accept
the other just
what am I saying
they never appreciated each other

Essay on the Inequality of Human Races

can you forget Adolf Hitler?

truly, impossible of the impossible,
I never understood
the people who don't see
the horrible common, characteristic of man
        the ephemeral
        of its absurd life
and discover differences
being full of hatred
differences
in the colour of skin or
in Religion

Clearette

when captain Heracles
with his ship
brings me to Preveza

to the dark gate of the castle
that leads from the harbour
to the central street
with the tower and the clock

the colourful group
of gypsy girls

the ovens that shine
at the far end
of the dark bakeries
and the standing golden loaves of bread
on the long counters
in the low-display windows

and the many roses
roses everywhere
in the orchards
climbing on the fences
the front steps of homes —

where are the crows
the poet saw?

Here Heracles saw the light
for the first time

since I started with Heracles
the proud lion
of freedom
Moutsanas
Odysseus Androutsos

Impossible to Serve Two Masters

waving the kerchief
do we welcome
those who come
or we greet
those who leave?
if the night follows
the day
surely the day
will follow the night
do the same leaves
the trees had last year
will also have
this spring?
Does the sky always end
on the same horizon?
A theory
or undoubted acceptance?
From crazy people
and kids
we learned the truth
that the logic people
and the old
hid

tell me how many nostalgic men
seek to return
but they finally didn't
so that they wouldn't feel nostalgic again?

Horn

in Constantinople mercilessly blows
the north wind Carayallis*
like the Vardaris* does in Thessaloniki
where they build most of the houses
out of wood
so that they may be a little warmer in the winter
and the people don't freeze

alas though in the middle of summer when
the eggplants appear and the panfrying starts
and the barbeques
only one spark is enough for the big
devastating fires to burn day and night
the houses tumble into ashes
endless black disasters turn
the big cities
into destruction zones

these people, surely Hellenes,
to find a solution
to the heavenly sent, and often repeated,
godly destruction
remember their ancient myths
that suit them, especially the myth of Phoenix
that rose from the ashes
brand new like before

---

*   *Names of winds*

R e s u l t: my father was born in Constantinople
a beautiful statue of Pavlos Melas was erected
in a beautiful square and
I know of someone; do I know him —
who knew in Constantinople,
among other things and adventures
a beautiful oleander (tree)
in its glory and its bitterness

and to bring back to his memory that oleander
every evening, he goes to have a glass of wine
at the grocery store
of Kahrimanis in Psyri
(Which Papadiamantis frequented)
and whispering he passionately sings
with the Asia Minor bouzouki player
accompanying him with the bouzouki
(of Papadiamantis)

Pandoras Box

Cogito, ergo sum
          Cartesiaus

History!
What unchecked information did it retain
what erroneous gossip passed to us!
A lot of bad luck and plots
ah, Cleo, surely recorded everything she heard.
It seems she didn't care
to sense
what truth was
and what wasn't?
A whole life of study and attention and research
allows us today
to discover, to claim that
everything about Pandora
and her box
are tales unworthy of mentioning.
Neither Pandora nor the gods
put anything in that box
nor did its opening
let the gifts escape
(they didn't exist)
Pretentious lies (cheap lies)
made us believe
that something was in
Pandora's box!
And if we act like morons
naïve men
(I first)

I'm in a position today
to confirm
that a box
belonging to Pandora
never existed.

Vincent Cornaros

As if the shortness
of life
wasn't enough
they often
made it
and without any reason
unbearable

and for this reason
I go around
from difficulty
to difficulty
and unhinged,
I sing

The Pain of Love

as her hair fluttered
in front of my eyes
suddenly
as if I woke up
and saw her
for the first time
I noticed
the beautiful
young
girl

I was touched by
the harmony
of her movements
her lissome
body
her attractive
eyes
the soft roundness
of her breasts
all the grace
rising
from her nice
fresh
being

and at once I thought
and philosophized
my mind went
to the unfortunate

who one day
will suffer
his martyrdom
and will suffer
when he will imagine
that this ethereal
being
has soul
and thoughts

and his heart will bleed
and he'll feel desperate
because he thinks
the small cranium
of hers
only has a tiny
spec of brain

Goalpost

He heard the bells tolling
and the vibrations of the bronze
that pierced the clear
Sunday morning
air

he wondered why the tolling
will there be followed
by hymns, joy and songs
or machine guns will echo
horribly
spreading
destruction
all over?

I'm only saying this:
we'll all run
to the goalposts, boys
to the goalposts
in vigil
sleepless guards
always ready
glancing here and there
be prepared

that the goals
won't start
like rain
and we'll be defeated

To Constantine Bakeas,

who paid attention to my latest poems

Indeed
my poetic production
as of lately
is truly
inexistent

not that I have stopped
writing
and reciting to myself
poems
verses
and fairytales

but as I forget
to write them
I forget them
and naturally
I have nothing to show

besides no one is asking for them:
I noticed how little attention
people pay
to poems

for a future thinker
my old poems

will be enough
and how talkative
my present silence
will be

Café Koutroumpas

not even the flat-footed
nor Soltatos from Anogeia
or Spiro Louis from Marousi
didn't ever ran so fast
as I did
I the writer
to get away
from people
who lie

some good-mannered commentators
explained by behaviour
in many ways,
usual story,
but nothing!
For me the most important
goal ultimately
was
to get away
from people who lie

Sequence

12
midnight
who knocks
at the door
this time?
Is it the Muse
luxuries
or the red-haired girl?
I open
yet
nothing
no one

I turn
miss Marika
the daughter of the good hymnist
of the parish
she discloses to me:
yes
it was the sea
it was the wind
it was the love of the captain
that stirred
my viscera

Berutiano

(Let's not forget of Alfonso Allais)

I am flabbergasted by this girl's vast knowledge! Is she
from Cairo or Alexandria? I'd lie to you. Regardless, as she
says, she completed her fine education in one European
college (catholic of course) in Cairo or Alexandria. With
such dedication and endless information, she talks of
the teaching personnel and what she owes to them. Pere
Magannat, mere Aklantan (Ann Merntez) and mere
Vitsialis. The brother d' Aisance! Fils Tik, doesn't hesitate
to add continuously and she teaches me of Europe with all
its secrets and details, true European, even though she's an
Afrikaner.

Orpheus

Nothing ever consoled Orpheus
for the double loss
of Euridice
sometimes, in his grief,
he'd sing a song for a while
other times, again for a short time,
he'd be enchanted
by the colours
and their many variations
and by chance
combinations

once, during a sundown,
he noticed beautiful lines
of clouds
against the light blue of the sky
like those about which
a cop in Kavouri, once,
as if regretfully cried out
these are the clouds of Engonopoulos

yet these, indeed,
weren't the clouds of Engonopoulos
but knives
blades
sharpened blades and scimitars
the toughest virgins of Thrace held
over their light blue bras

and brandishing them
in their hands,
the tough virgins
I say, fell over him:
they slithered him
they cut Orpheus
to pieces

About the Dryads

I face the poplar tree
from my window
I love it

for years now, winter or summer, I keep an eye on it
from close up
sometimes full of foliage
other times with its dry branches
in the north winds

but I've never seen its dryad
that must live in it
although I paid much attention
and looked at it for hours
I never stopped
to observe it secretly

perhaps there weren't any dryads
although no one
ever claimed so

perhaps my dryad
died years ago
perhaps, for years now,
she was added
to the merciless
and so unbearable absences
around us

About the Winds, Waters and Others

The autumnal
wind blows
and sweeps
the courtyard
dry leaves
that fell from the trees
the ripped letters
rags
lust
hope
dreams

sometimes the wind blows
and opens holes in the water
from which the tears
of fish rise
and flowers
loaves of bread
lust
hope dreams

and other times
and not in long-gone times
it charged under the long skirts
of beautiful girls
and reached up to
their secret
tender beauty

Angry Poem About the Occupation

Don't tell me the Kouroi that adorned the Hellenic shores have abandoned this forsaken place. This land, this black land, thousand times embittered never stopped to give birth to brave men. Even if we shed tears, we mourn their loss and are joyous for having them as our brothers. Who shall cry for the death of so many brave men? I shall cry and narrate their glory, but now I sing for Mitsos Asteriou, the eagle of Roumeli Tower of Atalanta, the brave, the manly, is among the first brave men of justice and freedom. His heart was as big as the mountains and his mind as high as the cypresses. Workers, let go of the tools let go of the hammers and with both hands show your contempt for the fascists, the lawless perverts who swore to the night that surrounds them, to enslave the World and spread darkness. And now tighten your fists, raise them high let us all together sing the song of the workers' victory: and behold, Mitsos is walking on earth. His face is pale, his lips embittered although benevolence always shines in his eyes. He's the one who believed, who was full of love look at how he extended his bloodied hands to us to hold us tightly onto his ripped chest.

To the wall they brought him blindfolded to be killed to the place they leaned his kind body the stones shed tears and wail like ghosts and an eagle, Hellenic eagle, flies over there and shades the black place with his wings and constantly groans, exhumes bitterness and curses.

About Crocodile Cladas

Who was Crocodile Cladas?
Was he a real crocodile
and his cries were false
through the night?
No, he was an eagle
and truly cried
in the night

(I mean during the night
and about the night of slavery
that mercilessly, and bitterly choked
the whole country)

yet his cries were his relief
tears that stopped
the longing and hope since dawn woke
inside of him
to throw everything down
and to spread
his wings

and with the joy of a graceful sun
he'd fly slowly and proudly
and he'd punish the slow and timid
and he'd spread freedom's messages
to the rightfully born souls

he didn't say stupidities, like others,
but he only repeated the holy word
Freedom

and he didn't care if during the sundown
the sun would find him
dead or alive
because the sun would find him
an eagle
among the trees
free of bonds
and for ever and ever

Esther Bessallell

And Esther
She's coming now...the poor
           Alberto Savinio, *Lorentzos Mavillis*

when I'll return
from Hell
to Thessaloniki
I won't let my beloved Hebrews
drive me crazy again
with the words
did you meet Solomoniko, in such a regiment
did you meet Moses, in such a company
such platoon or
perhaps you met Abraham somewhere? ...
and other things

I shall grab them by their faces
the naïve grieved people
and with shouts and cries
I'll insist that they tell me
if they met somewhere
little Esther
baby Esther
the bright star
of my early erotic years
my childhood

oh, the gift of the big Parisian bookstore
the trendy French girl
(Yet, with deep roots
in Canaan)
oh, the beautiful magnolia
the snow-white gardenia
my white jasmine
with her velvety
Spanish
eyes

Oh, the poetic echo
of bridges over the Sen
the bushy bloomed chestnut
of the magical avenues
the enchanting wistaria
of the palatial parks
the most thoughtful
exquisite harp of David

and how I lost her
the unimaginable happiness
through my fingers
life's whims were the reasons

I recall her
everywhere I go and
I always think of her
and my mind always brings me
close to her

perhaps she emigrated, as she longed for,
to Eretz Israel
perhaps the horrible Nazis
made a flower of her
or she now wilts somewhere
and doesn't
remember of me

Dione

men long for beauty
women constantly offer it
we know this
we
the descendants of the Marathon fighters

so, there is no reason
for a woman's year
and other such foolish acts
and masquerading
of the feminists

from the Glory to the Virgin Fighter
to the Cretan *mantinades*
to the Alphabet of Love

from the legendary phallic dances of the ancients
to the
these black eyes
that look at me
please lower them, my light...
they convince everyone
about the truth of the above

with words and deeds
we all compose bright bouquets
and endlessly
offer them
to women

More or Less

No, a good miner
doesn't hide
deep into the bowels of the earth
the whole truth
each secret
every solution

everything must be said
everything must come to light
so that, we erase it from the dictionary
the two insignificant
useless and hollow words
the *forever* and the *never*

and to finally
decide once and for all:
the flesh, yes, is willing
but the mind
sometimes, alas,
is weak

fairies
and trees
on the twilight
and the anchors
of the trumpeter

Readjustment

"Milen Demontzo, Zero Lemotzoglou" This was the signal and second signal of that year. Let it be so, the forgers could see it, and so could the pimps and rough neo-Babylonians, again in their lives, smart eyes. Flowery breasts of girls under traditional bras, strange memories of tears and moans, alabaster candelabras, bygone cascades of flowers (narcissuses), crystal carafes, exquisite, some with milk, others with sperm, or blood, offerings to the memory of old and new surrealists. And the passion remained a passion. And the poet is always ready, arms ready, to tell the truth, and to console. And the men from Mani were there, the ancient rocks too, and the guitars the bridges, the glasses and the rivers to the end, to the moment when everything ended. The band.

Startling

love
like life
is a dream

a handful of sand
that even if you hold it so tightly
it slips through the fingers
it escapes and falls
on the ground

the only steady:
the exquisite
the admirable
the fleeting miracle
of the rosy netting
and the black hair

the blood?

The Ballad of Sideris Isidor Steikovich

Isidor Sideris Steikovich
was the guard of my father's home
and remained devoted
to him
for all his life
(Only, that sometimes they, lightly, argued
about insignificant things of age:
who of the two was older)

Sideris, from Croatia, thought
of himself as a true Hellene and
brought piles of newspapers
to the house, so someone
would read them to him
since he couldn't
read at all

as time passed Sideris' snow-covered hair
made him colour his mustache
the naïve citizens used to say
that he went to the painting place

he limped a little too on his right leg
since believing in the cries for justice and freedom
of the neo-Turks
he took part
in the usual bloodbaths

to make his living
he did anything he could find
from mason to painter to welder
jack of all trades
even as a caretaker of high buildings

however, each Sunday he put on
his clean clothes
and shone as
he walked all over
smelling various colognes
(was a lover of the opposite sex too)
with his red cap
which he'd take off
as he entered the church

he claimed that his Bulgarian mother was a witch
something naturally impossible
to confirm
but I can say one thing
with certainty:
Sideris Steikovich was
a magician
among great magicians

what endless tales
of Nasreddin Hodja
he knew
other times he sang fanfares and
marches of the tactical Turkish Army
their passionate tunes
other times he described impressive events

of the daily life
with artistic passion

but he was one of the important painters

with the fabulous figures of Farber # 2
his hands created
he moistened the point of his pencil with his saliva
for his extra dark tones and
with bright oil paints, he painted on satin
exquisite beauties
flowers and
mermaids
(these were his favourites)
and I stole paper from my parents' visiting cards
the paper was always scarce

when I was a child, and they took me to the Polis
I passionately ran
to meet Sideris
and enjoy his magical
graceful charismas

since that polite and awe-inspiring
Sideris
was indeed my great teacher
along with Parthenis and Kontoglou
which I had
to mention

Adelais

The opposite in the science of super sensitivity
               is love
the opposite of sensitivity, also love
certainly, the endless longing in the life of a lonely
               joy.
Add the eyes: a myriad of eyes
piles of eyes
endless pairs of eyes, each of them
with its colour, glance, tongue
their vocabulary
their laughter, tears, sadness, lust
or even their indifference.
Wide open eyes, closed, eyes we keep, secretly
               obviously,
inside our eyes, always, always.
Women's eyes, the eyes of birds, children's
eyes we haven't seen yet they told us a lot
               about them
shining eyes, sleepy, eyes full of lust:
sparkling stars, super brilliant, endless on
our tender night sky.
Yet: kissing the eyes is not a separation.

Life, knowledge
knowledge of life (especially of the eyes)
is it a sign of a soft dream
or a delirium?

I'm referring to
seers to whom
the priests of the temple refer to
life (glory) of the eyes

Belisarius

as the holy empire groaned
under the suffering
when the nation bent under
the attacks of the barbarians
and the whole state kneeled under the endless
enemy strikes
they always seek him
to save the country from the suffering
they hoped for the saving
and salvation of the land
from him

and then?

afterwards
they didn't know him

thus
during the last years of the `30s period
among
the vague plans of philosophers
who were raging, despite their poor tools
for a possibly better predominance
and the immature, salivating, beggars and thieves
        of glory
the young Belisarius started
along with Andreas Embiricos
to create and
to live

The Valley with the Rose Gardens

What is life that isn't an enigma
            and a riddle?
However, is life a riddle and
            an enigma?

how unfortunate it is for the technocrats
who in the blindness around them
remain
true to their hollow beliefs
persistent
spiteful
opposing

the poet
the only, by God, salvatory solution
consolation
is the valley with the roses
or even
translated into
the valley of the rose gardens

Nikos Engonopoulos

Biography

Hellene surrealist painter and poet Nikos Engonopoulos
is one of the most well-known modern Hellenic painters
internationally. He was an important figure in the Generation of the '30s, a prominent group of artists and thinkers
in Hellas. The group was fascinated with Hellenic identity
and formed a Hellenic modernist movement in the wake of
Modernism's emergence in Europe and the turbulent period
after the population exchange between Hellas and Turkey
which caused many to consider serious questions regarding
culture and identity. This group includes some of Hellas's

most prominent poets, artists and writers, including Giorgos Seferis, Odysseas Elytis, and Yannis Tsarouchis.

The painter was born in Athens, on October 21, 1907, but he attended school in Paris and spent much of his childhood there. When he returned to Athens, the painter and poet worked several jobs, such as translator, bank teller, and secretary at the University of Athens. In 1930, the artist began working as a designer for the Urban Planning Department of the Hellenic Ministry of Public Works. Unsatisfied with his career and hoping to pursue art, Engonopoulos enrolled in the Athens School of Fine Arts in 1932, which was a vibrant period for the school during which many great Hellenic artists studied and taught.

While he was a student, the painter studied under great Hellenic painters, such as Konstantinos Parthenis and Fotis Kontoglou. He also met a few prominent artists and painters during that period, including the surrealist poet Andreas Embirikos and painters Yannis Tsarouchis, Giorgio de Chirico, and Yannis Moralis. While studying, Engonopoulos travelled to Paris, Vienna, Munich, and around Italy for artistic inspiration. When he returned to Hellas, and after graduating, the artist began teaching painting, art history, and scenography at the Polytechnic School of Athens.

Many of Engonopoulos's early works were painted using tempera on paper and described traditional Hellenic houses in bright colours. As his artistic vision developed, he focused on ancient Hellenic history and mythology, placing well-known figures from myth into strange and unexpected circumstances or physical forms. During his career as a painter, the artist also began writing surrealist poetry, which is considered some of the best in modern Hellenic literature.

In the late 1930s, Engonopoulos released his two earliest books of poetry, *Don't Talk to the Driver the Driver* and *The Clavichord of Silence*, both considered classics of modern Hellenic poetry. His most well-known poem, "Bolivar," was published in 1944. It was inspired by the Bolivian revolutionary leader Simon Bolivar, who helped free much of Latin America from Spanish colonial rule. Hellene composer Nikos Mamangakis set the poem in music in 1968. The song features Engonopoulos himself reciting the poem.

Engonopoulos has risen to great prominence in Hellas and abroad since the 1950ies. He was chosen to represent Hellas at the 27th Venice Biennale in 1954, where he displayed seventy-two paintings. Engonopoulos has been honoured in Hellas and internationally for his paintings and his poetry. His works are presented in the National Gallery in Athens, and museums, galleries, and private collections across Hellas.

The great poet and painter passed away in Athens in 1985 after suffering a heart attack.

https://Hellenicreporter.com/2022/10/11/
Hellenic-surrealist-nikos-engonopoulos/

Manolis Aligizakis

1947-

Emmanuel Aligizakis, (Manolis) is a poet, author, and translator. He's the most prolific writer-poet of the diaspora with over 90 books published in more than a dozen different countries and eleven languages. When he was eleven, he transcribed the nearly 500-year-old romantic poem Erotokritos, now released in a limited edition of 100 numbered copies and made available for collectors of such rare books at 5,000 Canadian Dollars: the most expensive book of its kind to this day.

He was recently appointed as an honorary instructor and fellow of the International Arts Academy and awarded a master's in the Arts in Literature. He is recognized for his ability to convey images and thoughts in a rich and evocative way that tugs at something deep within the reader. Born in the village of Kolibari on the island of Crete in 1947, he moved with his family at a young age to Thessaloniki and then to Athens, where he received his Bachelor of Arts in Political Sciences from the Panteion University of Athens.

After graduation, he served in the armed forces for two years. He emigrated to Vancouver in 1973, working as an iron worker, train labourer, taxi driver, and stockbroker, and studied English Literature at Simon Fraser University. He has written three novels and numerous collections of poetry, which are steadily being released as published works.

His articles, poems, and short stories in Greek and English have appeared in various magazines and newspapers in Canada, the United States, Hungary, Slovakia, Romania, Australia, Jordan, Serbia and Greece. His poetry has been translated into Romanian, Swedish, German, Hungarian, Ukrainian, French, Portuguese, Arabic, Turkish, Serbian, Russian, Italian, Chinese, and Japanese, languages, and published in book form and magazines in various countries.

He now lives in White Rock and spends his time writing, gardening, travelling, and heading Libros Libertad, an unorthodox and independent publishing company he founded in 2006 to publish literary books.

Following the steps of El Greco, he finishes all his books with the phrase: *Μανώλης Αλυγιζάκης, Κρης, εποίει*

His translation book "George Seferis-Collected Poems" was shortlisted for the Greek National Literary Awards the highest literary recognition of Greece. In September 2017 he was awarded the First Poetry Prize of the Mihai Eminescu International Poetry Festival, in Craiova, Romania.

His "Tasos Livaditis – Poems, Volume II" translation was long-listed for the 2023 Griffin Poetry Awards.

Shortlisted for the 2024 Zbigniew Herbert International Literary Awards in Warsaw, Poland.

After the release of Camouflage, his fourth poetry book, translated into Romanian by Larisa Caramavrov, the International Academy of Craiova awarded him the Special Poetry Prize of 2024 and named him its Cultural Ambassador.

BOOKS by MANOLIS ALIGIZAKIS

THE INCIDENTALS, poetry, Ekstasis Editions, 2024

SAVAGES and BEASTS, novel, Libros Libertad, 2024

WHEAT EARS-SELECTED POEMS, poetry, Libros Libertad, 2022

SWAMPED, novel, Ekstasis Editions, 2021

RED IN BLACK, poetry, Ekstasis Editions, 2019

THE QUEST, novel, Ekstasis Editions, 2018

THE MEDUSA GLANCE, poetry, Ekstasis Editions, spring 2017

THE SECOND ADVENT OF ZEUS, poetry, Ekstasis Editions, spring 2016

CHTHONIAN BODIES, paintings by Ken Kirkby and poems by Manolis Aligizakis, Libros Libertad, 2015

IMAGES OF ABSENCE, poetry, Ekstasis Editions, 2015

AUTUMN LEAVES, poetry, Ekstasis Editions, 2014

ÜBERMENSCH, poetry, Ekstasis Editions, 2013

MYTHOGRAPHY, paintings and poems, Libros Libertad, 2012

NOSTOS AND ALGOS, poetry, Ekstasis Editions, 2012

VORTEX, poetry, Libros Libertad, 2011

THE CIRCLE, novel, Libros Libertad, 2011

VERNAL EQUINOX, poetry, Ekstasis Editions, 2011

OPERA BUFA, poetry, Libros Libertad, 2010

VESPERS, paintings and poems, Libros Libertad, 2010

TRIPTYCH, poetry, Ekstasis Editions, 2010

NUANCES, poetry, Ekstasis Editions, 2009

RENDITION, poetry, Libros Libertad, 2009

IMPULSES, poetry, Libros Libertad, 2009

TROGLODYTES, poetry, Libros Libertad, 2008

PETROS SPATHIS, novel, Libros Libertad, 2008

EL GRECO, poetry, Libros Libertad, 2007

PATH OF THORNS, poetry, Libros Libertad, 2006

FOOTPRINTS IN SANDSTONE, poetry, Authorhouse, Bloomington, Indiana, 2006

THE ORPHANS, poetry, Authorhouse, Bloomington, Indiana, 2005

TRANSLATIONS FROM HELLENIC TO ENGLISH

YANNIS RITSOS-POEMS, Selected Books, Volume V, translated by Manolis Aligizakis, Libros Libertad, Surrey, BC, 2025

UGGA, poetry by Christos Tsiailis, translated by Manolis Aligizakis, Libros Libertad, 2025

ENTROPY, poetry by Vasilis Faitas, translated by Manolis Aligizakis, Libros Libertad, 2024

ANTONY FOSTIERIS-SELECTED POEMS, translated by Manolis Aligizakis, Libros Libertad, 2024

TWELVE NARRATIVES OF THE GYSPY, by Kostis Palamas, translated by Manolis Aligizakis, Libros Libertad 2024

YANNIS RITSOS-POEMS, SELECTED BOOKS, VOLUME IV, translated and introduced by Manolis Aligizakis, Libros Libertad, 2023

TASOS LIVADITIS-POEMS, Volume II, translated by Manolis Aligizakis, Libros Libertad, 2022

ELEGY POEMS, poetry by Thanasis Frontistis, translated by Manolis Algizakis, Haris Patsis Publishing Co, Athens, Hellas, 2021

YANNIS RITSOS-POEMS, SELECTED BOOKS, VOLUME III, translated by Manolis Aligizakis, Libros Libertad, 2021

TITOS PATRIKIOS-SELECTED POEMS, translated by Manolis Aligizakis, Libros Libertad, 2020

YANNIS RITSOS-POEMS, SELECTED BOOKS, VOLUME II, Translated by Manolis Aligizakis, Libros Libertad, Vancouver, BC, 2020

KATERINA ANGHELAKI ROOKE — SELECTED POEMS, poetry translated by Manolis Aligizakis, Ekstasis Editions, 2019.

NEO-HELLENE POETS an ANTHOLOGY of MODERN GREEK POETRY 1750-2018, poetry translated by Manolis Aligizakis, Ekstasis Editions and Libros Libertad, 2018

KARYOTAKIS — POLYDOURI, The Tragic Love Story, poetry translated by Manolis Aligizakis, Libros Libertad, 2016

HOURS OF THE STARS, poetry by Dimitris Liantinis, translated by Manolis Aligizakis, Libros Libertad, 2015

HEAR ME OUT, short stories, by Tzoutzi Mantzourani, translated by Manolis Aligizakis, Libros Libertad, 2015

CARESSING MYTHS, poetry by Dina Georgantopoulos, translated by Manolis Aligizakis, Libros libertad, 2015

IDOLATERS, a novel by Joanna Frangia, translated by Manolis Aligizakis, Libro's Libertad, 2014

TASOS LIVADITIS-SELECTED POEMS, translated by Manolis Aligizakis, Libros Libertad, 2014

YANNIS RITSOS-SELECTED POEMS, translated by Manolis Aligizakis, Ekstasis Editions, 2013

CLOE AND ALEXANDRA-SELECTED POEMS, translated by Manolis Aligizakis, Libros Libertad, 2013

GEORGE SEFERIS-COLLECTED POEMS, translated by Manolis Aligizakis, Libros Libertad, 3rd Edition, 2021

YANNIS RITSOS-POEMS, translated by Manolis Aligizakis, Libros Libertad, 2010

CONSTANTINE P CAVAFY-POEMS, translated by Manolis Aligizakis, Libros Libertad, 2008

CAVAFY-SELECTED POEMS, translated by Manolis Aligizakis, Ekstasis Editions, 2011

LONGHAND BOOKS

EROTOKRITOS, by Vitsentzos Kornaros, (rare book-collectible), transcribed by Manolis Aligizakis, Libros Libertad, 2015

Μανώλης Αλυγιζάκης, Κρης, εποίει

www.ingramcontent.com/pod-product-compliance
Lightning Source LLC
Chambersburg PA
CBHW032207030726
47494CB00020B/644